TROUBLE IN PARADISE

Christie looked at Jana critically. "Why are you talking about Marco so much all of a sudden?" she demanded. "Have you forgotten all about Randy?"

"Of . . . course not," Jana fumbled.

"So, why do you care, Christie?" asked Beth. "Unless, of course, *you* have a crush on Marco."

Christie felt her face turning red. "I was just asking. You're the one who said you thought he'd be a big star someday, Beth. Maybe *you've* got a crush on him."

"Just because I said he's a good singer doesn't mean I've got a crush on him."

"You've all been acting kind of funny," said Katie.

"*We* have?" asked Melanie. "What about you? You've never been interested in taking walks by yourself before. Where do you go anyway, Katie?"

"Wait a minute," interrupted Jana. "We're here to have fun, not to argue. Why's everyone getting so upset?"

The Fabulous Five stared at one another uneasily. . . .

THE FABULOUS FIVE

Caribbean Adventure

BETSY HAYNES

A BANTAM SKYLARK BOOK®
NEW YORK · TORONTO · LONDON · SYDNEY · AUCKLAND

RL 5, 009–012

CARIBBEAN ADVENTURE
A Bantam Skylark Book / December 1990

ISBN 0-553-15831-7

Published simultaneously in the United States and Canada

Bantam Books are published by Bantam Books, a division of Bantam
Doubleday Dell Publishing Group, Inc. Its trademark, consisting of
the words "Bantam Books" and the portrayal of a rooster, is Regis-
tered in U.S. Patent and Trademark Office and in other countries.
Marca Registrada. Bantam Books, 666 Fifth Avenue, New York,
New York 10103.

PRINTED IN THE UNITED STATES OF AMERICA

OPM   0 9 8 7 6 5 4 3 2 1

Caribbean Adventure

CHAPTER

1

*J*ana Morgan, Beth Barry, Katie Shannon, Christie Winchell, and Melanie Edwards talked excitedly and buckled their seat belts as the flight attendants hurriedly walked up and down the aisles checking to make sure everything was ready for landing. The Fabulous Five were sitting in a single row across the center section of the big DC-10 airplane.

Melanie glanced across the aisle at her mother, who was adjusting the seat belt of her little brother, Jeffy. Her father sat directly behind them in an aisle seat and was stuffing the travel brochures he had been reading during the entire trip from Kennedy Airport in New York back into his carry-on bag. It must be the

1

zillionth time he's read those, thought Melanie. Even though it was nighttime, she couldn't resist another glance toward the oblong windows of the aircraft. Below she could see the lights of the island of Barbados lying like twinkling diamonds on a black velvet cloth.

Melanie sighed and sank back in the seat. She would never forget the day her father had come home from work waving his arms excitedly and yelling at the top of his voice:

"I WON! I WON! I WON!"

He had grabbed Mrs. Edwards around the waist and swung her around the kitchen, singing loudly, "We're going to Barbados! We're going to Barbados!"

"What are you talking about?" Mrs. Edwards had asked, and then he explained that he had won a vacation to Barbados, an island in the Caribbean Sea, for being the best salesman in a contest his company had conducted. All expenses would be paid, and the family would be staying in a three-bedroom villa at The Caribbean Sands Village.

Melanie's mother dug out her calendar, and they gathered around the kitchen table, deciding to take the vacation during the school break between Christmas and New Year's, instead of waiting for summer vacation. They'd planned to leave on Christmas day. That way they would be able to get a whole week of vacation and fly back on New Year's Day.

Melanie told the rest of The Fabulous Five about the trip at school on Monday.

"That's great," said Katie. "But it'll cost you. You'll have to bring us back souvenirs."

"And postcards," said Christie. "I want a postcard from you every day."

"We're going to miss you," said Jana. "I can't imagine Christmas break without you to hang around with."

"Gosh, you're lucky," chimed in Beth. "Wouldn't it be neat if we could *all* go to Barbados?"

Then The Fabulous Five started talking about how much fun they could have together on a Caribbean island, sunbathing, waterskiing, and swimming in the ocean.

As her friends talked excitedly, Melanie looked around at their faces. She really wished they could go along.

That evening, she and the rest of her family were looking at brochures about Barbados.

"The beaches look great," she said sadly. "I wish The Fabulous Five could see them, too." Melanie nearly fell out of her chair at her mother's reply.

"I don't see why they couldn't come along, if their parents don't mind their leaving on Christmas day and they can afford the airfare and some money for meals," Mrs. Edwards said. "We'll have a three-bedroom villa with lots of space. And since there's maid service, I won't have to pick up after all of you. We can get a rollaway, and Jeffy can sleep in our room. What do you think, Larry?" she asked her husband.

"Sounds all right to me," Mr. Edwards said absently as he thumbed through a flyer. "You know I think we need to get a camcorder for this trip. Then we can enjoy it over and over again."

Melanie dashed upstairs to call each of her friends and tell them the news.

Christie had talked to her parents and called Melanie right back to say she could go. It had taken a couple of days for Jana's mother and stepfather and Beth's family to decide if they had the money to spare, and almost a week for Katie's mother, Willie, who was a widow and worked as a free-lance writer, to figure out how they could afford it. But eventually it was decided that they could all go.

Melanie took the travel brochures over to Jana's apartment one Saturday so they could all read about Barbados.

"It says it's the brightest jewel in the Caribbean," said Beth with awe in her voice.

"And listen to this," said Katie. "'This enchanting island has satin-white beaches, crystal-clear waters for diving, windsurfing, waterskiing, and para-sailing, and the lilting sound of Caribbean music is always in the air.'"

"And get this," cried Jana, "there are all kinds of shops where you can buy things duty free for about a third of what they cost in the United States. I'm asking mostly for money for Christmas, and I'm going to do some serious shopping."

"I read that you can wear shorts all year round in Barbados, and tennis is really popular there," said Christie. "That's my kind of place."

"Do they speak English in Barbados?" asked Beth with a worried look on her face.

"My father told me it was an English colony until 1966," said Melanie. "He's becoming a walking encyclopedia on Barbados. He also said we have a distant cousin living there. An Englishman named Milton Edwards."

Jana looked nervous. "What about passports? Do we need them to get into Barbados? Do we have enough time to get them, if we do?"

Melanie suddenly felt like an expert on travel to Barbados as the other girls turned to her for an answer. "No, we won't need passports. My father says we'll need copies of our birth certificates to prove we're United States citizens, and my mother wants each of your parents to write a letter giving her and my father permission to take you to a doctor or hospital if you get hurt." That sounded easy, and the girls went back to making their plans for the vacation.

As the trip to Barbados drew nearer, it was all The Fabulous Five could think or talk about. Each of them put every penny she could scrounge or earn from baby-sitting into her savings for the trip. They had tried promising each other they wouldn't talk about the trip for five whole minutes at a time, but someone had always blown it.

"We will be landing at Grandley Adams International Airport on the island of Barbados in approximately ten minutes," a flight attendant announced over the public address system. "Please fasten your seat belts and put your seats in an upright position."

Melanie did as she was told as the sound of the engines changed and the airplane got ready to land. We're almost there, she thought happy. This would be her very first time on a tropical island, and she couldn't wait to see what kinds of adventures were in store for The Fabulous Five.

The motor van drove through narrow streets crowded with small houses and pulled to a stop in the driveway of a beautiful hotel. While Mr. Edwards paid the driver, Mrs. Edwards, The Fabulous Five, and Jeffy jumped out.

"Where's the snow?" Jeffy cried. "It's sure hot here, like summer."

Melanie gave him an exasperated look. "We *explained* all that to you, Jeffy. It's summer here all the time."

"Oh, yeah," said Jeffy with a grin. He turned to watch two uniformed bellboys come down the hotel steps, open the back of the van, and start taking out luggage.

"Jeez, look at that," said Katie, staring straight up with her mouth hanging open. "*Real* palm trees. I never thought I'd see them in my whole life."

"And smell that ocean breeze," said Christie. "I can't *wait* to go swimming."

"*Everybody* to the ocean!" yelled Melanie, reaching for a bag at the curb in which she had packed her swimsuit.

"Wait a minute! Wait a minute!" commanded Mrs. Edwards. "*No* one is going anywhere until we've checked in and have all our things in our villa. *Then* we'll think about looking the place over together."

"Aw, Mom," said Melanie.

"Don't 'Aw, Mom' me," her mother said. "We're going to be here for seven days, and you'll have lots of time to enjoy yourselves. Right now we're going to get organized, and *you're* going to help."

"I'll help carry," said Jana, grabbing a small bag out of the back of the van.

"We'll take care of things, miss," said one of the bellboys, smiling. "Why don't all of you go inside? We'll have your bags there momentarily."

Jana smiled back and followed Mrs. Edwards, who was heading through the big arched doors into an open-air lobby.

"Wow!" said Beth. "This is the first time I've been inside a building that's outdoors."

"Can you imagine if this place were at home?" Christie asked, wide-eyed. "Right now it would be full of snowdrifts."

They all giggled and then looked around. The registration desk and gift, clothing, and souvenir shops were under a roofed area, but the opposite side was completely open over an outdoor swimming pool.

Across the pool from where The Fabulous Five stood gawking at their surroundings, guests sat at candle-lit tables in a restaurant with a thatched roof and sides that opened onto an outdoor dance floor. A young man was singing a calypso song to the ringing sounds of a steel band as dancers swayed rhythmically to the music. The low rumble of surf tumbling onto the shore came from the dark beyond the deck railing.

"I've died and gone to heaven," said Christie.

"Me, too," Katie said in a hushed tone. "Would you look at that Christmas tree."

The others followed her gaze to a large tree beside the registration desk where pastel lights twinkled softly in the branches.

"Oooooh," said Melanie, acting as if she were going to faint. "All the ornaments are seashells. It's gorgeous!"

After Mr. and Mrs. Edwards completed the check-in, the two bellboys led them to their villa. It was like a small house set among other small houses with sidewalks connecting them. Bushes with huge red and yellow flowers surrounded the villa, and clusters of palm trees stood in the grassy areas between the buildings.

"It's everything I ever dreamed of," cried Jana as she bounced up and down on the bed in one of the bedrooms.

"I'm so glad to be here. It's really great that your mom and dad let us come along, Melanie," said Katie.

They decided that Jana and Katie would share the smaller bedroom and Melanie, Christie, and Beth would take the larger one, and they quickly began to unpack.

"Did you see the beach right outside our patio doors?" called Jana, loudly enough to be heard in the other bedroom. "We can go for walks and hunt for shells before breakfast, even."

"Let's get our stuff hung up and go back to the lobby," said Beth, opening a suitcase.

"Yeah," agreed Melanie. "I can't wait to meet the guy who was singing with the band."

"Oh, no," cried Katie. "Here she goes again, ladies and gentlemen. Melanie Edwards has barely set foot on the island of Barbados and she's already scouting out the local boys."

"The singer's too old, Mel," said Jana. "I don't think he'd be interested in a bunch of junior high school girls."

"That's for sure," agreed Christie.

"I'm not down here to meet any boys," called Beth from the closet, where she was hanging up clothes. "I'm just going to enjoy myself as much as possible and then go home to see Keith."

"Me, too," said Jana. "I told Randy I'd write him a letter every day."

"I promised Tony I'd buy him a necklace with a piece of black coral on it," said Katie. "It'll look great with his black hair."

Melanie shoved her suitcase under the bed. "Come on, you guys. We can unpack later. I can't stand it anymore. I want to listen to the band and then walk on the beach."

"Me, too," said Christie. "Let's go."

As The Fabulous Five crossed the deck to the area under the thatched roof where the tables were located, they passed in front of the band. The singer was swaying rhythmically to a fast-beat calypso song, and Jana was startled when he nudged her gently and winked. She could feel heat running up her neck and into her face. She quickly ducked her head and hurried after the others.

I'm glad I was last in line and no one else saw that, Jana thought. She'd been so embarrassed, she reacted just like a little girl. You're thirteen, she told herself angrily, *not* a little kid.

After The Fabulous Five found a table, Jana looked back at the singer. Was he looking at her? Well, she told herself, the next time she got close to him she'd act more grown-up.

As the rest of The Fabulous Five ordered tropical juice drinks from the waiter, Beth sat back in her chair to enjoy the show. How old was the guy who was singing? she wondered. He looked about eighteen.

He was dressed in white pants and a bright green shirt with a cream-colored, palm-leaf pattern. Beth smiled to herself. Katie's boyfriend, Tony Calcaterra, would love that outfit. He tried to act so macho sometimes.

The singer had jet black, curly hair. His teeth were so clean and sparkly he must brush them with sand, Beth thought, and giggled to herself. He was definitely good-looking.

She stopped in mid-giggle. He was looking right at her, and his dazzling smile seemed to throw off sparks from the spotlights that shone on him. Was he intentionally looking at her, or did it just seem that way?

A few minutes later, the band took a break. The band members left their instruments on the stage and started mingling with the crowd.

Beth watched as the singer talked with an older couple sitting not far away. There was an interested expression on his face and he made lots of gestures with his hands. Boy, he really knows how to work the audience, thought Beth.

As the singer leaned forward to say something to the people, he turned his head and caught Beth staring at him. Slowly, he grinned, and she felt tingles run up and down her body. She had to struggle a moment before she was able to pull her eyes away from his.

"I'll be right back," said Christie, hopping out of her chair. "The waiter didn't bring me a straw."

Christie wound her way through the tables to the waiters' station. She waited while a waiter filled his tray with an order. She was just about to ask him for a straw when he turned in the opposite direction and left.

Suddenly she felt someone standing behind her. Thinking it was another waiter, she turned around and looked up into the shining black eyes of the singer from the band.

"Oh . . . excuse me," she said. "Am I in your way?"

"No, not at all," he responded in what was the most wonderful voice she had ever heard.

The eyes looking down at Christie made her feel as if she were going to melt into her shoes.

* * *

"I can't believe it," said Katie. "Look who's following Christie to our table."

The other girls whirled around. Christie was winding her way back from the counter with the singer right behind her.

"This is Marco Montavo," she said hesitantly as she reached the table.

"Welcome to my island." Marco flashed a smile around the table. "Do you mind if I sit down?" He pulled a chair up next to Katie before anyone could respond.

"Christie tells me you just got here. I'm sure you're going to have a great time."

Marco chattered away, telling The Fabulous Five about the fun things there were to do on Barbados.

"What do you do besides sing?" asked Beth.

"Oh, lots of things," Marco answered. "I take people on sight-seeing trips, I sell rides on my Jet Ski, and I teach people to dive. Anything to make money."

Then he told them how his grandparents had come from Spain to Barbados years ago and he had lived on the island all his life. He said that he was sixteen.

As Marco talked, Katie couldn't take her eyes off him. His hair was jet black, his eyes glittered, and his smile was dazzling. He looks a little like Tony, thought Katie, only older.

Then she noticed his shirt, which was green with palm leaves on it and was open at the front. A silver chain hung from his neck, a huge piece of black coral on the end of it.

I wanted to bring Tony a piece of black coral just like that, Katie thought. She shook her head without realizing it, trying to clear the confusion from her mind, and Marco looked at her curiously.

For the rest of the time he was at their table, Katie tried unsuccessfully to listen to what he was saying. Instead, all she could do was think to herself that Marco was the best-looking guy she'd ever seen.

Melanie thought she would faint right then and there when Christie brought Marco over. She put on her brightest smile, and then, remembering one of the tips for flirting she'd read about in a magazine, she looked deeply into his eyes.

"You're really a super singer," Melanie said, leaning as far as she could toward Marco. As she was thinking about whether it would be too obvious if she leaned closer, her elbow hit her knife and fork and they clattered to the floor.

"Whoops," she whispered, bending down to pick them up. She could feel her face turning bright red.

"Thanks," said Marco, looking at her curiously.

Marco stayed at The Fabulous Five's table until the band began getting ready to play again. When he got up to leave, his smile bathed each of The Fabulous Five once more before he turned and left five astonished girls staring after him.

CHAPTER

2

Melanie and Beth whipped the covers up and down so hard on Katie and Jana's bed that they billowed in the air.

"Wake up! Wake up! Wake up!" they shouted. "The tide's out, and we can look for seashells."

Katie opened one eye and squinted at the clock on the bedside table. "It's only six A.M.," she moaned.

Beth dove onto the bed between Katie and Jana. "The sun's been up for ages. Are you guys going to sleep the whole day away?"

"Beth and I have already been down to the beach," said Melanie as she climbed onto the bed and settled cross-legged at one corner. "The water's gorgeous, and there are shells all over the place from last night's high tide."

"Where's Christie?" asked Jana, shoving the covers back and swinging her feet to the floor.

"Putting on her swimsuit," responded Melanie.

The Fabulous Five's first morning on Barbados was even better than they had imagined when they were making their plans in the cold grayness of winter at home. They went swimming in the surf and walked along the beautiful stretch of white beach until the sand dwindled away at the base of a high cliff.

As the girls strolled back to the hotel, they stopped at a Jet Ski and surfboard concession. A Bajan boy who was working there yelled, "Hey! Rent a Jet Ski. We'll teach you how to use them."

"We'll be back," Christie promised him. "I definitely won't leave without trying one."

Farther along, they stopped to watch a young couple who looked like newlyweds push a small sailboat into the water and drift out to the horizon.

"Oh, that's so romantic," said Melanie, looking starry-eyed.

"It sure is," agreed Jana. "I feel like we've come to paradise."

Back at the hotel, the girls bought straw mats at the gift shop and spread them on the sand not far from their villa. Then they smeared sunscreen on their legs, and each other's back, and stretched out to sun bathe.

When lunchtime came, they swarmed back into the kitchen at noon complaining they were starving to death, Mr. Edwards announced that he had already called in their orders for lunch.

"We're having flying-fish sandwiches, french fries, and milk shakes," he said.

"Flying fish!" the girls cried in unison.

"Eeee-*yew!*" said Jana, making a face.

"What on earth is flying fish?" asked Melanie.

"It's a small fish that jumps out of the water and skims along the surface. It's also the national dish of Barbados," said Mr. Edwards. "Now, quit making faces. You like shrimp, don't you? And blackened red-fish?"

The girls nodded.

"Well, now you get to try flying fish. You're going to love it," he assured them.

It seemed like no time at all before a waiter came, carrying a huge tray high over his head. He arranged lunch for them on the table on their private patio, and the girls sat down, eyeing the sandwiches suspiciously.

"They look like regular fish sandwiches," ventured Katie.

"They smell okay, too," said Jana.

"Oh, come on, guys," said Beth. "Where's your sense of adventure?"

Beth took a big bite and chewed it slowly while the others watched her anxiously.

"Terrific!" she declared, and one by one the others tried their flying-fish sandwiches and agreed.

"I could definitely get used to living like this," said Jana, scooping up the last french fry on her plate and popping it into her mouth.

"Me, too," said Katie. "I feel like a queen."

"I knew I was really meant for a life of leisure," said Christie. "I've totally forgotten about math and history classes and working at the homework hot line."

After lunch, The Fabulous Five built a huge sand castle that came up to their waists next to the water. Then they went back into the water and took turns climbing onto each other's shoulders and trying to knock each other over. Exhausted, they plopped back down on their mats.

"You know, one thing I've noticed about this place," said Beth, "is that there don't seem to be any kids our age."

"You're right," said Melanie. "I haven't seen any either."

Christie rubbed some sunscreen on her legs. "Not right around here," she said. "But that doesn't mean there aren't any around."

"We didn't see any on the beach this morning, and there weren't any last night on the veranda when we went to watch the band, either," said Katie. "In fact, the only boys we've seen were working at the Jet Ski and surfboard concession stand."

"What about Marco?" asked Beth. "He's almost the same age as we are."

"He's sixteen," said Christie. "Sixteen-year-old boys don't pay attention to thirteen-year-old girls."

"But he doesn't know we're thirteen," said Melanie, giving the others a sly look. "And he won't if no one tells him."

"So who's going to tell?" asked Beth.

"Not me," said Jana, giggling.

"I wouldn't tell him for anything in the world," Christie added.

"Nobody tells, then," said Melanie. "Is it a deal?"

"It's a deal!" the others said in unison.

Jana got to her feet. "I think I'll go write postcards to Randy and Mom and Pink."

"I think I'll write postcards, too," said Katie.

"I'm going to change into my tennis clothes and go over to the courts," said Christie, brushing the sand off her mat. "Maybe I can find someone who wants to play."

Beth and Melanie decided to stay right where they were, lying in the sun with their dark glasses on and their noses heavily coated with white sunscreen.

Christie absently plucked at the strings of her racket as she looked around the courts. Two of the four courts were occupied. On the court nearest her were two men, and on the far court she spotted an older couple, who looked as if they really knew how to play.

To amuse herself, Christie started hitting the ball against a practice wall. The courts were pretty far from the hotel and she hoped she hadn't made the walk for nothing. She had been concentrating on batting the ball against the wall for about a half hour when someone said, "Not bad. How about playing a set with me?"

Christie turned and found herself facing Marco Montavo. His smile was just as spectacular in the daytime as it had been the night before.

"Okay," Christie said, trying to sound casual. She

couldn't believe she was about to play tennis with the singer from the band. Her insides were quivering as she walked to the far end of the court and waited for Marco to take the cover off his racket.

When Marco was ready, he flashed another confident smile across the net at Christie. "Can I have a few warm-ups, or do you want to beat me quickly?"

It turned out that Marco was a good player. Christie, who prided herself on playing tennis well, found herself working hard to stay even with him.

"Super!" he yelled when she put a well-placed shot by him.

She beat the singer seven games to five the first set, and he won the second set six to four.

The longer they played, the less either of them said, and everything faded from Christie's mind except the *poc . . . poc . . . poc* of the fluorescent-green ball as they sent it zinging back and forth across the net. She was hardly aware that the other two couples had stopped to watch them as she concentrated on winning.

The third game was tied six all, then seven all, then eight all. Then Marco did something he hadn't done before. He double-faulted. After that Marco seemed to have a tough time placing his shots as precisely as before, and Christie quickly won the match.

"Bravo!" exclaimed Marco as he wiped his face with

a towel and came around the net to shake Christie's hand. "You are one *very* good tennis player."

"Thanks," said Christie. Coming from Marco, the praise felt wonderful.

He put his arm around her shoulder as they walked off the court. "Tell you what. I'm going to buy you a lemonade as your grand prize for beating the tennis champion of Barbados." His old grin was back. "At least when all the other tennis players are on holiday," he said, laughing.

They sat in the shade of a palm-frond umbrella at a nearby soft-drink concession stand, and she listened while he talked. He was so handsome that being with him made her feel a little uneasy inside. He was a lot more self-assured and seemed to know so many more things than Jon Smith and the other boys she knew back home.

As they talked, she told him about life at Wakeman Junior High and about The Fabulous Five, being careful not to mention that they were only seventh-graders. She found out that when he was younger, he had started doing odd jobs around the hotels on the island and had joined the band the year before. He loved entertaining and meeting people from the United States.

"I have to go now," he said, getting up. "I've got to practice a new song. We'll play tennis again, won't we?" He looked questioningly at Christie. "This time I promise not to fall apart at the end."

Christie nodded.

As he walked away, disappointment washed over her. She wished she'd had more time with him. Marco was the most exciting guy she'd ever met.

Melanie thumbed through the postcards in the rack at the gift shop. She found one card with a picture of a funny face carved out of a coconut that said, *You're always on my mind*. Who should I send this to, wondered Melanie, Scott Daly, or Shane Arrington? She'd known Scott since fifth grade, but she had a big crush on Shane and not long ago he'd asked her to go out sometime. They hadn't had their date yet, but she couldn't wait for it to happen.

Finally Melanie decided to send the coconut face to Shane, and she picked up a different card for Scott. Next she roamed around, trying to find a card with a lizard on it to send to Shane's pet iguana, Igor. Shane would love it.

As Melanie looked through the postcards, she saw the singer they'd met last night come into the shop. Marco Montavo had a towel around his neck and a tennis racket in his hand. His hair was curled in damp ringlets. He must have just finished a hard tennis game, thought Melanie. Gosh, he's handsome.

Forgetting about the card for Igor, she summoned up all her courage and walked over to where Marco was bent over a glass-topped counter. She pretended to be interested in the display case, while she sneaked sidelong glances at the singer.

"Thinking about buying some cigars?" he asked with a wry grin.

Melanie flushed. She hadn't realized that it was a cigar case she was looking into.

"Er . . . yes, I mean no," she stuttered, trying not to look as foolish as she felt.

She gave up trying to speak and just gave him a big smile. It was a mistake. As soon as Melanie's eyes met his, she couldn't pull her gaze away. Her knees went all wobbly. "I didn't think you looked like the type who smokes cigars," Marco said, breaking the trance.

He gave her a wink and picked up the change from his purchase. "I'll see you around," he said.

"Right," responded Melanie limply. Her reply seemed inadequate, but it was all she could manage.

"Okay, everybody," said Mr. Edwards. "If you look to the right, you'll see the statue of Lord Nelson. This statue was actually erected before the famous one in Trafalgar Square in London, England. By the way, this is called Trafalgar Square, too. Isn't that interesting?" he asked enthusiastically.

Mr. Edwards was so enthralled with the statue that he didn't see The Fabulous Five all vigorously shaking their heads no and looking at each other cross-eyed.

Melanie's father had rented a mini-moke, a big, four-door motorized cart with a canopy roof that had fringe all around the edges. He insisted they all go sight-seeing together. Mrs. Edwards, Melanie, and he, were in the front seat, with Jeffy on his mother's lap. Jana, Christie, Beth, and Katie were scrunched tightly to-gether in the backseat. The four of them had tried every way they could think of to sit comfortably, but Christie was getting a cramp in her long legs because of the way she had them twisted, and Jana's and Katie's sides hurt from being jostled against the doorframes. Beth was convinced she was going to become a hunchback because of the way she had to sit in order to give the others room.

"Hand me the camcorder again, Kathy," Mr. Ed-wards said to his wife.

"Is there any dull historical sight that we haven't seen?" demanded Melanie as her father took the cam-era and walked toward the statue.

"I doubt it," muttered Katie. "We've seen the parliamentary building, the prime minister's home, the docks with the steamships and fishing boats, and millions of churches—and your father's videotaped them all."

"There he goes, ladies and gentlemen," said Beth, sounding like a circus barker as they watched Mr. Edwards circling Lord Nelson with the camera. "The one and only man in the world who talks to his camera so much it's started talking back to him."

The rest of The Fabulous Five giggled.

"Look!" cried Jana suddenly, pointing toward a nearby street. *"Killer shopping!"*

Four heads turned in unison toward the line of shops with racks of clothes arranged in rows on the sidewalks in front.

"Wow!" yelled Beth. "Let me at 'em."

"Me, too!" said Melanie.

"Wait a minute! Wait a minute!" Mrs. Edwards called. "Where do you think you're going?"

"We're just going over there to look at the clothes and stuff. Please let us, Mom. Please, please," Melanie begged. "We can't take one more historical monument."

A look of sympathy came over Mrs. Edwards's face. "Go ahead," she said, "but stay together."

Before she could finish getting the words out, the five girls were streaking down the street.

"Look at this," said Katie, holding up a T-shirt at one of the stores. It was bright aqua with a huge white hibiscus across the front. "Wouldn't it be great to wear this to Bumpers on a Saturday night?" Bumpers was the fast-food restaurant back home where everyone from junior high school hung out.

"How about this?" asked Beth, grabbing a full skirt with red, yellow, and blue parrots and spinning around. "Dahlings," she said dramatically, "don't I look beautiful?"

They all laughed.

At last The Fabulous Five were having fun. They bought postcards and beach hats and T-shirts, and then things for their boyfriends. Katie purchased a necklace with a beautiful piece of black coral for Tony, and Jana bought Randy a cap that said BARBADOS on the front. Beth bought Keith a pair of fluorescent-yellow-and-pink shorts that came down to the knees; Melanie bought Scott a T-shirt with a surfboarder on the front; and even though they were only dating now and then, Christie bought Jon a comb made out of whalebone with a scrimshaw drawing on it.

When they finally arrived back at their villa later that afternoon, The Fabulous Five tried on all the things they had bought and then admired each others' gifts for the boys.

"Shopping was great," said Christie.

"It sure was," agreed Jana.

"Now if we can just avoid my father when he wants to go sight-seeing, we'll be all right," said Melanie.

"If we're going to do anything besides hang around here, we're going to have to get him to take us to some places," said Katie.

"You know, I saw a bicycle rental place right outside the gates," said Beth. "Maybe we can rent bikes and go some places by ourselves."

"Good thinking, Barry," said Katie.

Stretching, Jana asked, "What are we doing to-night?"

Melanie looked around the room quickly. The memory of Marco singing flashed through her mind.

"Oh," she said as casually as she could, "I'd just kind of like to hang around here at The Caribbean Sands Village. Maybe watch the band again. They're pretty good," she added.

Christie traced the pattern on the leg of her shorts with one finger. "That sounds like fun to me," she said.

Jana, Beth, and Katie said they thought watching the band would be fun, too.

CHAPTER

3

"The fire-eater and Bajan dancers were pretty good last night, but I would rather have listened to the band," said Christie as The Fabulous Five walked toward the hotel lobby the next morning. Marco and the band had had the night off and a substitute group had performed.

"Me, too," agreed Beth.

"Yeah, I like the limbo and other stuff the band does," said Melanie.

Suddenly Beth halted in her tracks, and Katie ran into her.

"What's going on over there by the pool?" Beth asked, pointing.

Christie shielded her eyes from the glare of the sun. "It looks as if they're giving scuba-diving lessons."

A small group of hotel guests were sitting along the far side of the pool listening to a man speak. He wore air tanks on his back, a mask, and fins, and was demonstrating the diving equipment.

"Let's go watch," said Jana. "It might be fun."

The man in the water was tall and trim and his silver hair contrasted sharply with his deep tan. Wrinkles were etched in the corners of his eyes and he had white sunscreen smeared on his nose. He nodded to The Fabulous Five as they moved behind the people watching him.

"Good afternoon, young ladies," he said with an English accent. "You're just in time. We were just beginning our instructions on scuba diving. The Caribbean Sands provides the lessons free, so join right in. I've already asked the others—have any of you used scuba gear before?"

The Fabulous Five shook their heads.

"Good. That makes us all even. I haven't either," he said in a teasing tone.

"As I was saying, my name is Captain Smyth. Let's talk about the diving mask first, shall we? You'll need to know how to keep the glass from fogging up." He spat into the mask and rubbed the saliva vigorously around with his fingers.

"*Yuck!*" whispered Beth. "Did you see what he just did?"

The other girls made faces as he dunked the mask underwater to rinse out the spittle and then slipped it on over his head.

Captain Smyth continued his instructions, showing the class how to clear the mask of water, how to strap the air tanks on their backs, and how to breathe properly by inhaling air from the tube attached to the tank and breathing out through the nose.

"Now," he said, "the next thing we have to do is get some practical experience. I've got two tanks, so you can all get a turn using them.

"And so that it won't take us forever to let everyone try out the equipment, I have an assistant. He'll be taking care of people using one tank, and I'll supervise the use of the other one. Ladies and gentlemen, my assistant, Marco Montavo," Captain Smyth said, gesturing to the back of the class.

The Fabulous Five's heads whirled around.

Marco waved hello to the crowd. He was wearing a pale blue bathing suit that set off his tanned body.

Christie blinked her eyes as if she couldn't believe

what she was seeing, and Melanie, Jana, Beth, and Katie just stared at Marco. He spotted The Fabulous Five
and let loose a laser-beam smile in their direction.

"I'll start with you," Captain Smyth said to the man
nearest him. "Marco, why don't you start with those
five young ladies in the back row."

"Gladly," Marco replied. "Girls, why don't we go to the
other corner of the pool where we'll have more room?"

"I'm not sure I want to take lessons, after all," said
Jana, looking nervously after Marco as he carried the
tank around the end of the pool.

"Sure you do," insisted Melanie. "It'll be fun. Come
on." She hurried after Marco.

The others followed.

"Why don't you go first," Marco said to Beth, who
had ended up closest to him. He put his hands on her
waist to help her into the pool. "You're Beth, right?"

"Yes," she replied weakly.

"Okay, Beth," he said with a reassuring smile. "Turn
around and let's put this tank on your back."

Marco held the tank as she slipped her arms into the
straps. Then he held the mask out for her.

"Spit in it," he ordered.

"Do I have to?" Beth asked, looking back at Melanie, Jana, Katie, and Christie, who were watching intently.

"Come on, just a little bit," he said, laughing.

Beth spit into the mask and then making a face, rubbed the saliva around on the glass the way Captain Smyth had demonstrated. Next she rinsed it with pool water and put the mask on. "I can't breathe!" she said, pulling the mask back off.

Marco chuckled. "Don't try to breathe in through your nose when you've got the mask on. Breathe *in* through your *mouth* and *out* through your *nose*. Here, let me show you." He took the mask and put it on himself.

"See?" he asked, breathing easily.

Beth nodded.

"Okay," Marco said, giving the mask back. "Now put it on and lower yourself into the water, breathing in through your mouth and out through your nose."

Little shivers of fear ran up Beth's spine as she did as she was told. Her eyes were wide as she sank slowly below the surface, and the bubbles climbed up the outside of the mask. She felt as if she were a goldfish being put into a tank.

Gradually, Beth realized she wasn't going to drown, and a little feeling of exhilaration went through her. She even looked around to see if she could tell which legs belonged to which of her friends. Christie's were easy; they were the long ones.

Before she could identify the others, she felt Marco's hands pulling her up. She broke the surface smiling.

"Way to go!" Marco said jubilantly. The way he said it made Beth glad that he was so happy with her. The rest of The Fabulous Five applauded loudly.

"That was great," cried Katie.

"Now," Marco said, "I want you to swim to the opposite end of the pool and back underwater."

"What?" asked Beth, her eyes opening wide in disbelief.

"You heard me," he said, laughing.

Beth kicked off from the end of the pool. At first she held her breath, but when she realized what she was doing, she tried to relax. Breathe in through your *mouth* and out through your *nose*, she told herself. She reached out with both arms and pulled herself through the water.

Before she knew it she had reached the wall at the end of the pool, and her self-confidence soared. Why, using breathing tanks isn't really hard at all, she thought.

"*Fantastic!*" yelled Marco as she broke the surface in front of him. He grabbed Beth in his arms and lifted her in a bear hug.

Thrills ran up and down Beth's spine.

* * *

"Let's take you next," Marco said, looking at Jana.

Jana moved timidly to Marco, hoping that he wouldn't grab her and hug her the way he had done with Beth. She'd be totally embarrassed.

Marco helped Jana put the tank on and then watched while she cleaned the glass in her mask. When she was ready, he gently helped her ease down into the water. Instead of letting her sink to the bottom the way he had with Beth, Marco kept his hands on Jana's arms. He seemed to sense that Jana wasn't as confident as Beth.

After a few moments underwater, Marco pulled Jana up. "Why don't you try swimming to the end of the pool now?" He put his hands on Jana's waist and gave her a gentle push.

Jana took her time, trying not to get nervous. Gradually, she felt more confident. Swimming with all the equipment on wasn't so hard after all. In fact, it was fun. Jana almost giggled with pleasure, but remembered just in time that she was underwater.

She touched the wall at the opposite end of the pool, turned, and pushed off with her feet. As she swam back, she realized that Marco was a good instructor. He'd made it easy for her to learn how to dive. She had obviously been mistaken about his being a total show-off. All entertainers have to try to look good in front of people, she told herself. Deep down Marco is a very sensitive person.

Marco was waiting for Jana when she got back to her starting place. Instead of picking her up and hugging her the way he had Beth, he gave her a wink that told her he thought she'd done a good job.

Jana gave him a big smile in return.

"Your turn," Marco said to Katie.

Katie braced herself and stuck out her chin as she waded over to him. She didn't like the way Marco seemed to think he could dazzle girls. Mr. Wonderful would just have to realize that all females weren't going to fall all over him. Especially not Katie Shannon.

Marco seemed to be assessing her as she approached.

"Here," he said, handing her the mask to clean.

When she had finished, he handed her the air tank and without a word, watched her put it on.

Katie glanced at Marco as she struggled to get the tank straps on over her shoulders. She had expected him to try to help her get it on, but he didn't. He must realize I can do it myself, she thought with satisfaction.

"Excellent," Marco said when she had finished and he had checked the straps' tightness.

In spite of herself, Katie felt a swelling of pride at his approval. He did truly look impressed that she could put the equipment on by herself and without any additional instruction.

Katie lowered herself underwater and swam to the opposite end of the pool and back.

"There's not much I can teach *you*," Marco said, nodding approvingly at her. He lifted the air tank off her back as she slipped out of the straps. This time Katie didn't mind the help.

"You really are something," Marco said softly from behind her.

Before she could stop herself, Katie jerked around and found herself looking into the deepest, darkest eyes she had ever seen. With an effort, Katie tore her eyes away, and she gave Marco a feeble smile.

Christie couldn't concentrate with Marco so close to her. It seemed as if no matter how she tried to avoid it, their fingers or arms would touch as he gave her the diving mask, helped her on with the tank, or gave her an instruction. Each time it happened, little thrills raced through her.

This is the same as learning something new in gym class, or from a tennis pro, she said to herself firmly. You always pick up things quickly.

But Christie couldn't seem to keep any of Marco's instructions straight. The first time she went underwater, she forgot to brush her hair back the way he had told her to, and water got into her mask. Then she almost panicked when she tried to breathe through her nose instead of her mouth and couldn't.

What in the world's wrong with me? she thought as she took her place back at the edge of the pool to let Melanie have her turn.

As Marco showed Melanie how to clean the mask and do the other things, Melanie listened carefully. When he asked her to swim underwater to the end of the pool and back, she thought about trying one of the fancy maneuvers she'd seen on television during the swimming events in the summer Olympics, but decided against it. Things were going too great, and she didn't want to ruin them by drowning.

When her turn was over, Melanie put her hand on Marco's arm and told him in the sincerest way she could how much she appreciated his teaching her to scuba. She knew by the twinkle in his eyes and the

way the corners of his mouth turned up in a smile that
he liked her.

That night Melanie lay awake in the bedroom she was
sharing with Beth and Christie. She knew they were
awake, too, but she didn't feel like talking. Instead she
wanted to think about Marco Montavo, the most wonderful boy in the whole world. She bit back a giggle as
she imagined being marooned on an island with him.
They could swim together in a beautiful blue lagoon,
and he would spear fish for food. Maybe they'd build a
thatched house and live in it together. She sighed with
pleasure at the thought. Maybe they would even refuse
to be rescued if someone found them.

In the bed next to Melanie's, Beth had her eyes closed,
but she wasn't sleeping. She was imagining that Marco
had come to visit her at Wacko Junior High, and she
was showing him around and introducing him to all
her friends. Boy, would Laura McCall be jealous!
Keith Masterson was a bit of a problem, but she had
gone with Keith since the sixth grade, and a person
couldn't be expected to go with the same boy her
whole life, could she? After all, one had to grow up.

*   *   *

I'm glad Beth and Melanie don't feel like talking to-night, thought Christie. I'm just not in the mood. She wanted to be left alone to think about Marco Montavo.

You're a tourist, she told herself, and Marco is an entertainer. He's just doing his job as an employee of The Caribbean Sands Village. Still she couldn't deny that he'd been awfully attentive. The way he had looked at her when they were playing tennis, and again today at the pool! Was he really just doing his job?

She sighed and rolled over on her side. One thing was for sure—she was developing a big crush on the singer.

In the next bedroom, Jana was tossing and turning. She couldn't understand her own emotions. Her boy-friend, Randy Kirwan, was the kindest, most sincere person in the world, and Jana had never dreamed of liking any boy besides him, but Marco made her feel totally confused. Jana pounded her pillow, wanting to go to sleep and quit thinking about the cute island boy.

Katie yanked at the covers that had gotten all mixed up on the bed she was sharing with Jana. What's going on with Jana tonight? she wondered. She seems so restless.

*   *   *

But Katie was having trouble sleeping, too. Her mind kept flitting back and forth between Tony and Marco. First, she would see Tony's face, and then she would see Marco's. Marco's too old for me, she told herself, trying to be rational. And Tony's a strong person who treats me like an equal. I don't want another boyfriend. But didn't Marco treat her as if he respected her, too? He hadn't tried to make her feel like a helpless female at all. But Marco lives here, and I live miles away, she thought. It was foolish to think that they would ever see each other again after this vacation.

All five of them tossed and turned into the night.

CHAPTER

"Well, how's everyone on this beautiful, sunny morning?" Mr. Edwards asked cheerfully as he came out onto the patio where The Fabulous Five, Mrs. Edwards, and Jeffy were having breakfast. He was wearing shorts splashed with bright colors, a green shirt, sandals over brown dress socks, and dark sunglasses.

Melanie took one look at the way her father was dressed and rolled her eyes at her friends in disbelief. Beth and Jana covered their mouths to stifle their giggles.

"Fine, Mr. Edwards," said Christie, holding a piece of toast in front of her mouth so he couldn't see her grin.

"Have you told the girls what's on the agenda for today?" Mr. Edwards asked his wife.

She shook her head. "No. Since you're the one who decided on our itinerary, I thought I'd let you do it, dear."

"Great!" he said rubbing his hands together. "You're all going to *love* this. There's going to be something for everyone. First, we're going to Gun Hill Signal Station, which is where the British used to look out for enemy ships. I was in the lobby a few minutes ago and heard all about it from that young singer. He said we'd love it."

At the mention of Marco, the girls' interest perked up for a moment. It died again an instant later.

"Next we're going to take a tour of Villa Nova," continued Mr. Edwards. "It's an old plantation house, and then we're going to Harrison's Cave. Doesn't that sound super?" He looked as if he thought they all should jump up and down with glee.

"Daddy!" wailed Melanie. "Can't you and Mom just go look for cousin Milton Edwards, or something? We just want to lie on the beach and go to the pool and do things like that. Can't we do what we want?"

"Melanie," Mr. Edwards said, "the best way to get to know a place is to see as much of it as possible when you first arrive. Yesterday we saw the largest city in Barbados, and today we'll see the rest of the island.

You'll thank me for this later when you can tell all your friends what you saw. They'll think you're a world traveler."

"I don't care if they think I'm a world traveler," responded Melanie. "I just want them to admire my tan, which I can get by traveling to that beach right over there."

"Don't be selfish, Melanie," Mr. Edwards insisted. "Think about your friends. You girls would like to see the island, wouldn't you?"

Jana, Christie, Katie, and Beth glumly nodded and avoided looking at Melanie.

"Traitors!" she muttered under her breath.

"What did I tell you, Melanie?" her father said. "Hurry and finish your breakfasts, girls. We've got a full day ahead of us."

The mini-moke jolted to a halt in the parking lot, and Christie slid out of the backseat. Looking around, she saw the lot was half-filled with cars, other mini-mokes, and a few motor scooters. Not far away on a hill stood a stone tower that looked like a miniature fortress. A line of tourists was making its way up the path that led to the tower. Christie fell in behind the others as they headed in that direction.

"We can't stay long if we're going to see everything," said Mr. Edwards, hoisting his camcorder up on his shoulder. "Everyone has to meet back here in fifteen minutes."

"It is beautiful," said Jana as The Fabulous Five stood on a parapet and looked out across the island.

"It's pretty on the beach by our villa, too," said Melanie grumpily.

"Oh, Melanie, don't be a spoilsport," said Katie. "Your father means well."

"Besides, he said we wouldn't have to go sightseeing much more," agreed Beth.

"Just wait and see," Melanie warned. "This week will be gone before we know it and we won't have had any fun."

"You're not the only one who wants to have fun," said Katie.

Christie sighed. She was tired of listening to the others squabble.

There were several old cannons poking over the fortress wall in the direction of the sea, and she decided to look at them more closely. As she walked along behind the cannons, she tried to imagine what it was like for a soldier who'd stood here three hundred years ago, watching for tall-masted ships on the horizon.

Beyond the wall were some steps leading down to

where beautiful red and yellow flowers were growing. She followed the path and found a place that was out of view of the others. She loved being with The Fabulous Five in Barbados, but she was still glad to have a chance to be alone for a few minutes.

The green land rolled away from where she sat to the white sand beaches in the distance. Beyond that, Christie could hardly tell where the clear blue sky met the water on the horizon. She had to agree with Jana, it was a breathtaking place.

"Mind if I join you?"

Christie jumped at the voice that came from behind her. Turning, she found Marco looking down at her.

"Oh . . . uh, no," she said, fumbling for words. "That's okay."

He found a seat on a nearby rock. "Beautiful view, isn't it?"

"I was just admiring it." Christie felt nervous with Marco sitting so close to her. "Do you come here often?" she asked quickly.

Marco plucked a blade of grass and nibbled on it. "Quite a bit. It's one of my favorite places. It makes me feel so . . . so at peace." He turned his dark eyes to her. "My beautiful island is like a mother to me. It warms me and feeds me and takes care of me. See those waves out there?" He pointed with the blade of grass toward the sea. "My island can also be very strong and stern when there's a storm. The waves come crashing in and the Bajan people are quiet like children with an angry parent."

Christie couldn't take her eyes off his face. What he was saying was so poetic. He really was sensitive. She had been mistaken when she thought that he was just a shallow show-business person who acted as if he were on stage all the time.

"Wow," she said. "That's beautiful."

"Thank you," he said, smiling appreciatively at her. He seemed to really mean it.

"Are you here alone?" he asked.

"No. My friends are up by the tower."

Marco looked in that direction. "Where are you going after you leave here?"

Christie laughed. "Melanie's father has everything planned. We're going to Villa Nova next, which he says is an old plantation. Then we're going to Harrison's Cave. He's going to keep us busy. We can only stay here fifteen minutes."

"You'll like those places," Marco said. "Are you going to them in that order?"

"According to Mr. Edwards. I don't think he'll let us get more than a minute off his schedule, either," she answered, giggling.

She looked at her watch. Rats, she thought, it's time

to meet the others. "I guess I'd better get back before everyone starts looking for me," she said reluctantly.

Marco reached out and took her hand. "I'm glad you like my hill. I'm glad you like my island."

She felt as if she were swimming in his deep, dark eyes. "I do," she said. "I do like your hill and your island. I . . . like them very much."

He squeezed her hand and then stood up. "I'll see you again," he said. "Soon." He turned to leave and then stopped. "One thing. Would you not mention our meeting to anyone? Employees of the Village aren't supposed to fraternize with the guests."

Christie nodded and he turned to go. She couldn't believe it. The handsome island singer must like her. Then another thought crossed her mind. Marco had been the one who had suggested Gun Hill Signal Station to Mr. Edwards this morning. Had Marco planned their meeting? Had he come to this spot just to see her?

"I have to admit, this is a fan-*tab*-ulous place," said Melanie as the Edwardses and The Fabulous Five toured the Villa Nova. It was a beautiful old plantation home, as Mr. Edwards had said it would be, with crystal chandeliers, antique furniture, and dozens of rooms. "It's so *romantic*," gushed Melanie.

"I'm glad you're enjoying *something*, Melanie," said her mother, who had a death grip on Jeffy's hand to keep him from crashing into one of the priceless antiques. "I thought you were going to pout the whole trip."

Melanie clapped a hand over her mouth. "I was going to."

"And now you've blown it," said Jana, laughing.

Melanie laughed, too. "Oh, well. I can't win them all. I'm going to see what's out behind the house. Anyone want to go with me?"

"Not me," said Katie. "I want to check out the bedrooms again. They're enormous. You could get six rooms the size of my bedroom into the smallest one."

The rest of The Fabulous Five shook their heads and followed Katie upstairs.

Outside, Melanie wandered through a garden with roses, hibiscus, bougainvillea, poinciana, and other flowers, some of them as large as small trees. She wandered up and down the garden rows smelling the blossoms and trying to tell the differences in their scents. Wouldn't it be great if we had flowers like this in the middle of winter back home? she thought. Remembering all the snow that had been on the ground at home made her feel even more glad to be on Barbados.

As she rounded a large pink hibiscus bush, she ran smack into someone who reached out and caught her to keep her from falling.

"Careful," said Marco, giving her a warm smile and holding her steady for a second.

"Oh!" said Melanie, trying to catch her breath. "It's you."

"I think so," said Marco, scanning his body. "Yep! It's me, all right."

Melanie laughed. "It's just that I didn't expect to see you here. Shouldn't you be back at the Village practicing, or something?"

He laughed and his eyes twinkled as they looked into hers. He leaned closer to her as he talked.

I think he's flirting with me, Melanie thought. Shivery tingles ran up and down her back at the idea of the handsome, sixteen-year-old singer's wanting to flirt with *her*.

"No," he said, "we don't have to practice every day. We pretty well know our routines. Actually, what are *you* doing here?"

"It was my dad's idea," said Melanie. "I'm glad he wanted to come now," she said. Marco looked at the flowers growing all around them. "This is my favorite place," he said. "I come here all the time."

"You do?" asked Melanie, raising her eyebrows. "I mean, uh . . . that's nice. I don't know many boys, er . . . guys," she said quickly, not wanting him to think of her as young, "who would like to come to a garden."

"Well," Marco responded, "it reminds me just how beautiful my island is."

"Oh . . . that's nice," said Melanie. He was so romantic.

"I was born on Barbados, you know."

"Yes, I know," answered Melanie, not able to take her eyes off his face.

"She's like a mother to me. She wraps me in her beauty"—he swept his arm around to indicate the flowers—"she feeds me, and her wonderful sun warms me. What more can I ask of her?"

Melanie could only nod. She knew she was staring at him with moon eyes, but she couldn't help it. He was awesome.

"I'm glad you like my garden," he said.

"Oh, I *do*! I *do*! I like your garden a lot," said Melanie, looking up at him sincerely. How could she not like the garden, especially with him standing in the middle of it?

"Melanie!" Mrs. Edwards called from the villa.

Melanie grimaced. *Not now!* she thought. Not when everything was going so great between her and Marco!

"I have to go," he said, backing away.

Melanie was furious that her mother had broken the mood. "But . . ." she started to say.

"I'll see you *soon*," Marco said, giving her his warmest smile. "Uh, one thing. Would you not mention our meeting to anyone? The Caribbean Village's management doesn't like for employees to mingle with the guests."

"Sure," said Melanie. She'd promise him anything.

"Wait up," Jana whispered to Katie, who was directly in front of her. The guide who was leading them through Harrison's Cave was moving along quickly, and Jana didn't want to get left behind. She had read stories about people who had gotten lost in caves, and sometimes it was months, even years, before their dead bodies were found.

"Well, hurry up," Katie complained. "I don't want to get left behind, either."

The tour group finally stopped and the guide continued telling them about the unusual formations of stalactites and stalagmites. "And over to the left," the guide was saying, "you'll notice the unusual wall that looks like the curtain to a theater stage. Isn't it beautiful?"

The wall was wet with moisture that ran down it from above and seemed to shimmer in the colored floodlights that were shining on it from several directions.

"If you want a closer look," said their guide, "you can move along the pathway to your left."

The crowd moved in that direction, which was where Jana and Katie were standing. The girls were pushed gently toward the edge of the rock formation.

"It is gorgeous, isn't it?" said Katie.

"Yeah," agreed Jana. "It's even prettier close up."

Jana moved farther along the edge of the path where the curtain of stone wrapped around a corner into a lit passageway. There she saw a stalagmite that looked just like Alf. She laughed and went over to it to feel its wrinkled nose.

When she turned to go back, she saw another formation that looked like Dopey from the Seven Dwarfs. And then there was another that looked like Sleepy. Giggling to herself, Jana went to see them closer.

Looking around the small room, she was surprised at how many faces she could see in the stone if she let

her imagination run free. She went from one to another looking at them.

"Look, Katie . . ." Jana started to say, but when she
turned around, she was all alone.

A wave of panic swept over her. "Katie!" she called.
There was no answer, and all of a sudden the dripping
of water in the cave seemed loud and lonely.

"Katie!" Jana ran in the direction from which she
thought they had come.

She stopped and looked around frantically. Why did
everything seem so different? Where was Alf? None of
the stones coming up from the floor looked anything
like Alf or any of the others she had examined.

Fear filled Jana's stomach. She was lost! She looked
in one direction and then another, but she couldn't find
her way out.

Panicking is *not* going to help, she scolded herself.
Stay calm. Use your head. Think!

"Hi!"

"*Eeeek!*" Jana jumped straight up in the air, and the
hair on the back of her neck stood out as if she had
gotten an electrical shock. Her heart was pounding as
Marco came out of a passage.

"Gee! I'm sorry!" he said, looking concerned. "I
didn't mean to scare you. Are you all right?"

Jana put her hand on her chest to try to slow her racing heart. "I . . . I think so," she said.

He put his arm around her shoulders. "Are you sure? *Man!* I didn't mean to scare you like that. Next time I'll honk when I come around a curve."

Jana giggled. "I shouldn't be so jumpy," she said, finally feeling calmer. "I guess I got lost and was panicking a little." Jana looked up at him. The worried look on his face showed just how concerned he was. She knew he felt badly about frightening her.

"What are you doing in here by yourself, anyway?" Marco asked.

"I came back to look at some of those things," Jana answered, pointing at the stones. "I didn't realize the others had left."

"No problem," Marco said. "I know my way around these caves. I'll take you to your group."

"You will? That would be great. Maybe everyone won't even have to know I got lost."

"It's our secret," Marco said, grinning.

"You must come here a lot to know your way around so well."

"I ride my motorcycle up here all the time. It's one of my favorite places. It probably sounds corny, but coming here kind of puts me back in touch with myself. It's so quiet and peaceful. You know how show business is, I need to get away from people sometimes, and it makes me feel more in touch with my island."

Jana looked up at him. He seemed so much more mature than any other boy she'd ever known.

He took Jana by the hand and led her through the tunnels until they could hear the guide's voice ahead of them.

"They're in that room, said Marco, pointing to an opening in the cave wall. "I think you can find them okay."

"You're leaving?" Jana asked.

"Yup. I've got things to do. See you later," he called, and then disappeared through an opening.

Jana tried to hide her disappointment as she turned and hurried after the tour group.

CHAPTER

5

*W*hy are Christie, Melanie, and Jana so quiet? mused Beth as Mr. Edwards guided the mini-moke through traffic on the way back to The Caribbean Sands Village. Christie had grown quiet at the Gun Hill Signal Station, and then later Melanie and Jana seemed to be lost in their own thoughts, too. Every time Beth tried to talk to them, the three of them just responded with absentminded smiles.

The trip down from the hills in the center of the island had been boring, except for Jeffy's bouncing from lap to lap and nearly falling out the open side of the mini-moke. After Katie and she had run out of things to say about the scenery, Beth had started looking around for interesting people to watch, which she loved to do. It was good for her training as an actress. But except for island ladies strolling along with brightly colored umbrellas and a motorcycle that followed them at a distance, there wasn't much traffic, and even people-watching had become dull.

"Here we are," said Melanie's father as he pulled up in front of their hotel. "Everybody out."

When they were back at the villa, Beth asked hopefully, "Does anyone want to go shopping? There are some cute boutiques just up the road."

"Not me," said Katie. "I don't have that much money, and I want to hold out for a while before I spend it."

"How about you, Jana?" Beth asked.

"Hmm?" replied Jana, as if she hadn't heard a word Beth had said.

Beth looked at Christie and Melanie. They were totally absorbed in their own thoughts. If they wanted to go along, they could say so. She wasn't about to ask them again.

"Well, *I'm* going shopping," she announced loudly, then left.

Beth's spirits lifted as she walked along the narrow street leading away from The Caribbean Sands hotel. Sidewalk vendors called to her, cheerfully trying to interest her in their fruit or straw hats or jewelry. The windows of the small shops were filled with brightly colored clothes and T-shirts with pictures of bright red hibiscus and beach scenes.

As she passed a shop called the Pelican's Roost, Beth saw a gorgeous swimsuit hanging in the window. It was fluorescent yellow and pink, with thin shoulder straps, and tied at the waist with a sash. Not able to resist, she went inside to find out its price.

"This would look *lovely* on you," said the clerk as she took the suit from the window. "And it's only thirty-nine ninety-five."

Beth gulped. It *was* beautiful . . . but $39.95? She held it up to herself and looked in a full-length mirror. It was more than beautiful, it was absolutely gorgeous. If her parents were here, she might be able to talk them into buying it for her as a belated Christmas present.

"*Perfect!* It's just right for you."

Beth looked up and saw Marco Montavo standing behind her in the mirror's reflection. His confident grin caused the blood to run up her neck and into her face.

"Oh, hi," Beth said.

"Hi, yourself," Marco said. "Seriously, that would look terrific on you."

"Do you get a commission on sales here?" Beth asked, laughing.

"Hey, I wish I did. But they wouldn't hire me."

"He's just teasing you, miss," said the clerk. "You can't believe a word the boy says. Marco comes in and harasses me and my customers all the time. He's just looking for something to do."

Beth smiled at the clerk and then turned back to Marco. "I'd hire you." His warm look made her feel good all over.

"I'll take the swimsuit," she told the clerk suddenly. What the heck, Beth thought. Marco likes it, and Laura McCall will probably commit suicide when she sees me in it next summer. Besides, Beth could tell the story about the handsome boy from Barbados who convinced her to buy it. She had to restrain herself from giggling at the thought, and it made counting out the money less painful.

"Going my way?" asked Marco as they stepped out of the store.

"Depends on which way you're going," responded Beth, flashing him a sly grin.

"Have you been to The Flying Fish yet?" he asked.

"The Flying Fish? I thought that was a sandwich."

Marco chuckled. "It is, but this particular Flying Fish is a restaurant. It's a great spot. Lots of people. Lots of things happening."

"Well, in that case, lead the way," Beth said cheer-fully.

The Flying Fish had an open deck built out over the water. Young people were sitting around eating and drinking soft drinks. Some were dancing on a tiny floor to music coming from an old Wurlitzer jukebox.

"That's amazing!" said Beth.

"What's amazing?" asked Marco, looking around.

"The jukebox. It's just like the one back home at Bumpers. That's one of the places we hang out. It has old carnival bumper cars that ki . . . *you* can sit in." Beth hoped he didn't realize that she had almost said "kids."

"Neat," said Marco. "There are a couple of tables over there by the railing."

Beth followed him through the crowd. The sight of the white sand and the sunlight playing on the waves almost took her breath away.

After the waitress had brought them two colas, Marco leaned back in his chair. "What did you do to-day?" he asked, eyeing her closely.

"We went to Gun Hill Signal Station, a plantation called Villa Nova, and some caves."

Marco stirred his soda with his straw and asked in a low voice, "What did you see there?"

Beth shrugged. "The caves were pretty interesting, but the rest of it was boring. You probably go to those places all the time."

For some reason, Marco seemed relieved at her answer. He waved his hand as if dismissing the idea. "No," he said. "I'm not really interested in that stuff either. I like to be where the *action* is."

"Me, too," agreed Beth.

Marco focused his zillion-dollar smile on her. "Okay, do you want to see what kind of fortune-teller I am?"

"Fortune-teller?"

"Sure," he said with a wink. "I can tell all about people. For instance, you like to do fun things."

"That's true, but most people do."

"Not everyone. And let me see . . ." He squinted his eyes as he looked at her as if he were analyzing her. "You also like colorful clothes."

"You know that from the bathing suit I bought," she said, laughing.

"You also want to be an entertainer."

Beth stared at him in amazement. "I want to become an actress. But how did you know that?"

It was Marco's turn to laugh. "I told you. I can tell fortunes."

"I don't believe you," said Beth.

"How about this? You would like people to pay more attention to you than they do."

Beth's mouth dropped open. That was definitely true. At home, her family never listened to her. There was always too much going on.

"You see, I'm right," Marco said with a chuckle.

"But . . ." Beth stuttered.

Marco put his hand on hers. "You and I are a lot alike, Beth. All I'm saying about you is what I know about myself. I like to be around people, and I'm an entertainer because I want people to notice me. You see, we're very much alike."

"Oohh," said Beth. "I *do* see." He was right. She and Marco were a lot alike. She could see it clearly now. It made her feel as if he really did understand her.

For a moment Beth and Marco looked at each other in silence, his hand holding hers.

Then he leaned closer. "Can I ask you a favor?"

"Sure," breathed Beth.

"It's about my job at the hotel. I'm not supposed to fraternize with the guests, but, with you . . . I can't help it. Would you not tell anyone we were together? Not even your friends?"

"Yes," said Beth in a tiny voice. She could hardly contain her glee.

He squeezed her hand. "Want to dance?"

Beth floated to the dance floor behind Marco with her hand still in his.

Later that afternoon, Katie walked along the water's edge by herself. She had gotten tired of hanging around the villa. Beth had come back from her shopping trip and had gone directly to her room. It had surprised Katie because Beth usually liked to show off the things she'd bought.

Christie was in the living room reading a book about the Caribbean that she had bought at the hotel gift shop, Melanie was watching a soap opera about a man and a woman who were deeply in love, and Jana was trying to write another letter to Randy Kirwan. Apparently Jana wasn't having much luck composing the letter. There were wads of paper all over the floor where she had tossed them before trying again.

Katie nearly stepped on a shell but jumped back as it skittered away on the back of a little hermit crab who was using it for a home. She smiled at the funny little creature and poked it gently with her finger to prod it to go back into the water.

As she waded out into the beautiful blue Caribbean, she saw a floating platform offshore with people standing on it, holding the edges of huge orange parachutes. They were para-sailing. Katie stood watching for a few moments as one by one each parachute filled with air and rose gracefully with a para-sailor dangling in the air below it.

Suddenly, Katie heard the roar of a motor. A Jet Ski was racing toward her. It turned just in time to avoid hitting her, but a wave pushed her backward, drenching her from the waist up.

"*That wasn't funny, you maniac!*" she yelled.

The boy on the Jet Ski headed slowly back toward her. To Katie's surprise it was Marco Montavo.

"Sorry!" he called as he rode the machine up onto the beach. He cut the motor and waded back to where Katie was standing.

"I really am sorry," he said. "Are you all right?"

"I'll survive, I guess. But you ought to be careful. If you ran over someone with that thing, they'd be fish food."

"I usually am careful, but the throttle stuck on me, and I was looking down to see what was wrong. I fixed it. Could I make it up to you by taking you for a ride?"

"Me?" asked Katie, surprised again. She looked at the Jet Ski sitting just out of the water. It looked as if it would be fun, but the idea of riding on it with Marco made her feel uneasy.

"Well, if you're afraid . . ."

Katie didn't let him finish the sentence. She could do *anything* a boy could, and lots of things better.

"Afraid! Why would I be afraid of that thing?" she asked, nodding toward the Jet Ski. "If you can ride it, I can, too."

Marco looked at her appraisingly. "I'm sure you can. Tell you what. You can even drive."

Katie's heart leapt into her throat. Drive the Jet Ski? I didn't mean I could do that, she thought to herself. Not without lessons, anyway. Why did I open my big mouth? I'll probably head straight out to sea and won't be able to turn the thing around. Great white sharks were probably out there just waiting for her. But she couldn't back down in front of Marco. It would be too humiliating.

"You'll have to show me how to start it," she said weakly.

"I have to do more than that. It would be downright stupid for me to let you go by yourself without some instruction. I'll go out with you and show you how to run it. Then when you're ready, you can take over. How's that for a deal?"

A huge wave of relief rolled over Katie. It was a lot better than her going by herself and never returning.

Marco gave her a life jacket to put on while he pulled

the Jet Ski back into the water. The two of them floated it far enough away from the beach so it wouldn't touch bottom.

After it was started and they were aboard, Marco headed it out gently to deeper water.

Katie hung on to his life jacket for support. She was just beginning to feel the whole thing was a piece of cake when Marco revved the engine and the Jet Ski jumped forward like a horse breaking out of a rodeo pen.

"*Yikes!*" yelled Katie, gripping Marco's life vest with all her might.

He reached down and pulled first her right hand and then her left hand around his waist. With her arms wrapped tightly around him, Katie felt a little uncomfortable but a lot safer.

Marco headed the Jet Ski out into open water and then turned to run parallel to the coast.

Away from the breakers along the shore, the water was smoother, and Katie gradually started relaxing. She even began to enjoy the ride as they skimmed along the surface of the water with the din of the motor enfolding them like a cocoon.

Marco tapped her hand and pointed off to the right. Two dolphins broke the surface in perfect unison. Marco nudged her again and pointed in front of them where a large manta ray rose out of the water and splashed back in. The ray wasn't as beautiful as the dolphins, but with its wide black shape it was awesome.

A lighthouse appeared on a point of land in front of them. "South Point," Marco explained over his shoulder. He turned the Jet Ski in a wide arc and headed back in the direction they had come from.

The wind blew Katie's red hair back from her face as they cruised along. At one point several small flying fish skipped along the water in front of them like birds skittering out of their way.

"Okay, your turn," said Marco as he brought the Jet Ski to a stop not far from the shore. He stood up and let her slide in front of him.

"All you have to do is turn that handle grip," he said, pointing. "Just take your time until you're comfortable with it."

Katie turned the throttle and they moved slowly forward. After they had gone a short way, she decided to try a left turn. It went smoothly, so she tried one to the right. It was like riding a bike, except you didn't have to pedal. *I can do this*, she thought. It's easy.

Katie twisted the handle grip farther, and the Jet Ski moved forward faster. She twisted it even farther, and the front of the machine rose and started skipping across the waves, sending spray in both directions.

She tried a few more cautious turns and then twisted the throttle as far as it would go. The Jet Ski jumped forward and she felt as if she were one of the dolphins she had seen playing in the surf. It was wonderful.

It was then that she became aware of Marco's arms wrapped around her. She had been so excited about driving the Jet Ski that she hadn't noticed before. She could even feel his breath in her ear. He was awfully close to her.

Finally, Katie guided the Jet Ski in toward the shore to the point they had started from.

"Get close in, and just as you're about to hit the beach, gun it," Marco instructed. "Take it in as far up as you can."

Katie did as she was told and beached the machine several feet out of the water.

"Great job!" said Marco, giving Katie a hug. "You're a pro already!"

Katie grinned, feeling herself blush.

Marco's face turned serious. "I'd like to ask you to have a soda with me, but I can't. There's a rule against employees fraternizing with the guests at The Caribbean Sands," Marco said. "You understand, don't you?"

"I guess so," Katie said, trying to hide her disappointment.

"I can't help it, though," he said, sounding almost angry. "I want to see you some more. . . . If it wasn't for that darn rule."

He hit one fist in the palm of the other hand. "I'll tell you what," he said. "If you can keep it a secret about you and me, I'll find a way for us to see each other. Can you do that?"

Katie nodded, not totally understanding why she did. After all, Tony Calcaterra was her boyfriend. Why did this singer from Barbados suddenly seem so important to her?

CHAPTER

6

"Does my hair look okay?" asked Beth. She had used mousse and brushed her short spikes almost straight up.

"It looks great to me," responded Jana. "How do I look?"

"Super," said Christie, putting a dab of cologne behind each ear. "Isn't that the dress you wore when you and Randy were chosen Mr. and Miss Seventh Grade?"

Jana flushed and looked away from her friend. "Yes," she answered with an embarrassed look. "It's the only dress I brought with me."

"It's funny how each of us decided to dress up tonight," said Beth.

"Is everybody ready?" asked Melanie.

"I still have to put on some eye shadow," said Jana.

"Well, hurry," said Melanie. "We're going to be late."

"I am hurrying," said Jana.

"My goodness, you girls look nice," said Mrs. Edwards when The Fabulous Five went out onto the patio where she, her husband, and Jeffy were sitting. "What's the big occasion?"

"Oh, no big deal," answered Melanie, shrugging.

"I don't know about everybody else, but I was getting tired of looking like a slob," said Christie.

"Me, too," agreed Katie.

"I bet I know!" said Jeffy. "They're going to see boys."

"Jeffy!" exclaimed Melanie indignantly. "There are *other* things to think about besides boys."

The other four girls' jaws dropped.

"What did you just say?" asked Katie, dumbfounded.

"Well, there are," said Melanie defensively.

"We know," Katie teased. "We just didn't think you knew."

Melanie stuck her tongue out at Katie.

"Well, have a good time," said Mrs. Edwards. "Don't be out late."

"Okay," Melanie said innocently.

*   *   *

"Let's hurry," said Jana, "before all the tables are taken."

"If you hadn't taken so long putting on your eye shadow, we wouldn't have to hurry," said Melanie.

"I wasn't the only one who was slow," Jana responded, glaring a little at her friend.

"Do you think the singer will be there yet?" asked Christie casually.

"What's his name?" asked Katie. "Marco?"

"I think that's it," said Beth. "Let's try to sit close to the band so we can see better."

"Good idea," agreed Melanie. "The steel drums are *so* fascinating." She hoped no one would ask when she had suddenly developed an interest in music.

As The Fabulous Five marched across the deck and passed near the band, each of them sneaked a look at Marco, hoping he would see her and flash a smile. But Marco was talking to one of the other musicians and didn't seem to notice any of them.

"Oh, great," said Melanie, shooting an annoyed look at Jana, "all the tables near the band are taken."

Jana frowned at her. "We'll just have to sit in the back."

"I can't see the band," complained Beth once they were seated.

"Don't worry," said Katie. "I'll let you know what they're doing."

"Besides," added Christie, "you'll be able to hear them."

"It's not the same," said Beth, folding her arms and slumping back in her chair.

They ordered sodas as the band started playing and turned to watch the musicians. Beth propped herself up on one leg so she could see.

The first song was "Puerto Rico," and The Fabulous Five rocked and swayed to its calypso beat. When it ended, they clapped louder than any other table in the place.

After a few more lively songs to warm up the crowd, Marco sang a slow ballad, "Your Love."

Each of the girls closed her eyes, thinking about the time she had spent with Marco earlier that day.

"*De Congaline*'!" yelled the band as soon as Marco finished singing. The musicians burst into a lively conga rhythm, yelling and making wild-jungle-bird sounds.

With a cordless microphone in one hand, Marco headed for the crowd, followed by two guitar players. All three of them were doing quick little conga dance steps.

The crowd cheered and several people got up, placing their hands on each other's hips, and forming separate conga lines.

Marco sang into the mike, "Let your body move . . . to de tune," and the people who were still seated started swaying and clapping their hands to the rhythm. As people jumped up from their tables, the separate conga lines started connecting to form longer lines.

The Fabulous Five were on their feet, clapping and swaying to the music, too.

As Marco sang, "Let your body sway . . . in this way," he moved toward The Fabulous Five's table and stood dancing in place. The line of people behind him swayed as he reached out and took Christie's and Katie's hands and they started doing the little conga steps with a guitar player strumming on each side of them. Then he took the hands of each of the other three girls in turn and they danced, too.

When Marco yelled, "*Limbo!*" the guitar players switched songs and everyone danced and clapped after him to the dance floor. Two waiters held a long stick shoulder high between them, and Marco led a woman in a yellow dress under it. Her husband followed her, and then other people from the audience joined in the fun.

When everyone had passed under the stick, the two men lowered it to their waists and the people started under it again, bending their knees and leaning backward. The Fabulous Five easily made it under each time. As the stick was gradually lowered to the level of the men's thighs and then to their knees, people dropped out until The Fabulous Five were the only ones left to try.

The crowd was gathered in a big circle and everyone was clapping. The band had moved in close, too, and the music got louder. First Beth slid under the stick, then Christie, then Jana, then Melanie, and then Katie. After each girl made it, the crowd applauded loudly.

The men lowered the stick again.

Beth looked at it, took a deep breath, and started under. The pole slid across her chest, but she slithered through without falling as Marco reached out and took her hand to help her.

As he pulled her up, he whispered, "Meet me at The Flying Fish tomorrow morning at ten o'clock. Don't tell anyone."

Beth looked at him in surprise, but she had to move on because Christie was coming under the stick.

Christie made it, too, and came up grinning as Marco reached for her hand and helped her up.

"Meet me on the tennis court at eight o'clock in the morning. Don't tell anyone," he whispered. He pushed her gently after Beth.

"Meet me at Sand Dollar Beach at one o'clock tomorrow," he whispered to Jana as he helped her, too.

Jana wondered if she had heard him correctly with the loud music and clapping going on. "What?" she asked.

"Meet me at Sand Dollar Beach," he whispered again, looking around anxiously to see if anyone else could hear what he was saying. "It's not far if you rent a bike. It's along the south shore of the island, and you'll know you're there when you see a big rock offshore. Just follow the path down to the water. Don't forget . . . one o'clock, and don't tell anyone."

Jana nodded as he hustled her to the side.

Melanie was thrilled to see Marco on the other side of the bar helping her friends. He seemed to be saying something nice to each of them because they were all smiling when they left him. The best part was that he would be there when she came through. She gave him a big grin as she came up after going under the bar and looked deeply into his eyes.

"Meet me in the gardens on the far side of the hotel at two tomorrow," he whispered.

"Okay," Melanie answered, surprised.

He gave her his fabulous smile. "Remember, don't tell anyone."

Going under the limbo pole was easy for Katie. She knew she could still do it even if they lowered the pole even more.

She stuck out her hands to balance herself at the last moment, and Marco grabbed them. A thrill ran through her, like the one she had had on the Jet Ski when he had his arms wrapped around her.

"Meet me tomorrow at three o'clock by the Jet Ski concession," Marco said. "I need to talk to you, but don't tell anyone."

"I will. I mean, I *will* meet you," said Katie, "and I *won't* tell."

The singing and dancing lasted for two more hours, and The Fabulous Five were all exhausted when they returned to their villa and pulled lounge chairs up in a semicircle on the patio so they could look out over the crashing waves at the shoreline. A full moon lighted the sea and silvered the tops of the breakers as they rolled in to shore. The soft, deep sound of the water lulled them as they lay silently with their thoughts. Each one was dying to tell her friends about her rendezvous with the singer. But there was still some tension between them, and besides that, he had sworn them all to secrecy.

CHAPTER

7

Christie dodged the slipper that sailed by her head and hit the wall behind her.

"What are you doing up so early?" grumbled Melanie, rubbing her eyes in disbelief.

Christie looked at her bleary-eyed friend and put a finger to her lips. "I'm going to play tennis," she whispered, trying not to wake Beth. "I thought I might find someone who needs a partner."

"*Nobody* would be dumb enough to get up this early after being out late, except Christie Winchell," said Melanie as she yanked the covers up over her head and burrowed down into the bed.

Christie smiled to herself. Only somebody with a

81

good reason, she thought. And Marco Montavo was a very good reason.

Christie was so excited she practically skipped down the street to the tennis courts. True to his word, Marco was waiting there for her.

"Hi!" he called. "I've been waiting for you for half an hour."

Christie looked at her watch. "But you said to meet you at eight o'clock. It's eight now."

He laughed. "I couldn't wait to see you, so I got here early."

They took opposite sides of the net and started loosening up by lobbing the ball casually back and forth. Marco moved gracefully from side to side, bending his knees to stroke the ball with the face of the racket at just the right level. Christie was watching him so closely that she missed returning the ball twice.

"Ready?" he called after they had warmed up for a few minutes.

"Ready," she called back.

They volleyed for first serve, and she won.

Her first two serves were faults, giving him the point. Instead of being angry with herself for goofing up, as she usually would be, she shook her head and just smiled at Marco.

Things didn't go well at all for Christie. She kept miss-ing easy shots, and Marco quickly won the first game.

As they started the second game, Christie hopped back and forth from one foot to the other, trying to loosen up and build her concentration. But when Marco served, Christie was watching him, instead of the ball, and she missed another shot.

"Sorry!" called Christie sheepishly.

For the rest of the game her shots didn't improve, but the score stayed close. All of a sudden she realized why she wasn't falling further behind. Marco was bag-ging it. He was intentionally missing shots so he wouldn't embarrass her.

No way! she thought angrily. I'm not going to have someone give me a game, and she smashed his return with all her might. Instead of going where she had aimed it, it went sailing over the fence.

"Way to go, slugger!" called Marco.

Christie laughed and then shrugged. "I guess I'm not on my game today."

Marco walked around the net to her side. "Well, you're certainly not playing the way you did the other day. Why don't we take a break?"

They put the covers back on their rackets, and she followed him off the court. He led her along a pathway that was lined with tall hibiscus bushes blooming with huge red and yellow flowers.

"You've taken a lot of tennis lessons, haven't you?" he asked.

She smiled. "Yes, I have. My father wants me to turn pro someday. But you couldn't tell it from the way I was playing this morning."

Marco smiled. "Hey, we all have off days. You ought to hear me when I hit a sour note singing."

At that moment Christie didn't care if she played tennis well ever again. The only thing that seemed to matter was being with Marco.

Beth slowed to a walk half a block from The Flying Fish. She had been afraid she'd be late because of having to share the bathroom with Melanie, Katie, and Jana. If Christie had been there, Beth would never have gotten out of the villa.

Beth glanced at her watch. She was ten minutes early. Good, she thought, I can put on some makeup. With the rest of The Fabulous Five hanging around the villa, she hadn't even been able to fix her hair. Beth dashed up the front steps and headed for the girls' room. Inside, she laid out her hairbrush, eye shadow, and lipstick along the chrome metal shelf under the mirror and carefully began putting on the makeup.

When she'd finished applying the makeup and brushing her hair, she stuffed her things back in her purse and took one last glance in the mirror. Not bad, she thought, surveying her reflection. She had on her favorite outfit, knee-length shorts that were sunshine yellow with five-inch bands of orange-and-yellow paisley print at the bottom of the legs. Jana had looked at her strangely when she put on the vest with matching paisley print. "Why are you so dressed up?" she'd asked.

"I'm just in a good mood today," Beth had answered quickly, sneaking the matching orange scarf into her bag to avoid further questions.

Beth took a deep breath and went out to the restaurant. On the outside deck several people were sitting around drinking coffee or sodas, but she didn't see Marco. The table they had sat at the day before was empty, and she took a seat. Good, she thought. Maybe he'll start thinking of it as *our* table.

A fresh cut flower was in a bud vase on the table, and she positioned it so that it was near her face, then carefully arranged her orange scarf so that it looked as if it had been casually placed around her neck. Next she tried sitting in different positions, trying to find the one that would have the most dramatic effect. She even sucked in her cheeks to give herself a more mature look.

Feeling as if she was as ready as she could get, Beth tried to hold the pose, peeking out of the corner of her eye every few seconds to see if Marco was coming. It seemed like a zillion minutes passed before he finally walked into the restaurant. Beth froze in position, trying not to wrinkle her nose at the scene in front of her—a sea gull eating a rotten fish.

"Sorry I'm late," said Marco. "I played tennis with a friend this morning and had to take a shower."

"No problem," Beth said in a chirpy tone. "I was just sitting here enjoying the scenery. As a matter of fact, I just got here myself."

"Good," said Marco. "I'd hate to leave someone as pretty as you sitting by herself for long."

Beth turned her head so he couldn't see her blush. Usually she could disguise almost any emotion, but hiding her feelings around him was almost impossible.

After the waitress had brought them their sodas, Beth asked, "What do you like to do?"

Marco looked thoughtful. "Oh, lots of things."

"Like what?"

"Like take my Jet Ski out to the *Peg Leg Pete* and sell rides on it to the tourists, and give scuba lessons."

"What do they do on *Peg Leg Pete*?" asked Beth.

"It's an old two-masted pirate ship. There are day trips on *Peg Leg Pete* off the coast of Barbados. On board there's dancing and entertainment, and when the ship anchors, somebody has to walk the plank. They usually pick someone like you," Marco added with a grin. "After that, you can go swimming and snorkeling, and there's even a rope so you can swing out over the water from the deck and dive in. They've got great food and lots to drink."

"Oh, that sounds like fun," said Beth. "I bet you go all the time."

A dark cloud seemed to pass over Marco's eyes. "No, not really. The *Peg Leg Pete* is for rich tourists like you. I'm usually in the water with the rest of the guys selling Jet Ski rides to all you pretty girls from the United States."

Beth bowed her head so Marco couldn't see her face. "Do you bring all those pretty girls to The Flying Fish?"

Marco threw back his head and laughed. "Oh, no! You're the only pretty girl I've ever brought here." For some reason he didn't sound sincere, but then his expression turned serious and he looked deep into her eyes. "You believe that, don't you?"

"Sure," she said, uncertain, but trying to smile.

"Good!" said Marco, looking pleased. "Now, enough of this. We're two wild and crazy people. Let's go have some fun."

"Great!" Beth laughed, forgetting her doubts. Marco really did like her. If only she could tell the rest of The Fabulous Five.

They walked hand in hand through the streets, looking in the shop windows. He bought her a piece of sugarcane, which looked like a bamboo stick, and showed her how to suck the sweet juice out of it. Everywhere they went, cabdrivers shouted hello at Marco, and he returned their greetings. Beth couldn't remember when she'd had so much fun.

Finally, Marco said he had something he had to do, and they walked back to The Flying Fish, where he had his motorcycle parked. He even had an extra helmet for her.

He pulled to a stop a couple of blocks from the Caribbean Sands. "I'm sorry, but I have to let you off here. My job, you know."

Beth slid off the back of the motorcycle and handed him the helmet. "It was fun."

"For me, too," Marco said.

Embarrassed at what she was about to say, Beth looked down at her feet. "I hope we can do it again."

Marco looked at her warmly. "Sure. We will. I promise. But right now I've got to get going."

Beth felt like jumping up and down. *He wants to see me again!*

When Beth walked into the villa, everyone was sitting down to lunch on the patio.

"Well, where have you been?" asked Mrs. Edwards. "You look awfully happy."

"Oh, just shopping," responded Beth as she took a flying-fish sandwich from the platter in the center of the table and avoided looking at her friends.

"Where's all the stuff you bought?" asked Christie. "You never come back from shopping empty-handed."

"I do, too," Beth protested.

"She's probably been sneaking around," said Melanie. "Bet if we looked in the closet we'd find all kinds of packages."

"Were you really sneaking around, Bethy?" asked Jeffy.

Beth blushed. She had been sneaking around. Not buying things, but sneaking around with Marco.

"Aha! She has been," said Katie. "I can see it in her

eyes. Okay, Beth Barry, where'd you hide everything?"

"I didn't buy anything," Beth insisted. "But if you don't believe me, look around. You can keep anything you find."

"Is that a promise?" asked Katie, her eyes gleaming.

"It's a promise," agreed Beth.

Jana, who hadn't said anything since Beth had come in, suddenly stood up. "May I be excused?"

"Why, yes, dear," said Mrs. Edwards. "You certainly didn't eat much. Have you had enough?"

Jana nodded. "I've had plenty. The flying fish sure fills you up."

"It does?" asked Mr. Edwards. The rest of the group looked at Jana.

"Where are you going?" asked Christie. "If you wait up, I might come with you."

"I'm just going to walk around," Jana said, looking nervous. "It'll probably be boring so why don't you stay here."

Jana hurried out of the room before Christie could reply.

CHAPTER

8

*J*ana pedaled the rented bike along the highway, looking for the large rock out in the water that would tell her she had found Sand Dollar Beach. It was a beautiful day, and she was glad to be meeting Marco, but she also felt uncomfortable about slipping away from her friends. She was also worried about Randy. What would he think if he knew she was sneaking off to meet a sixteen-year-old boy?

He'll never know, Jana vowed silently. After all, I'll be back home next week, and I'll never see Marco again. Besides, she thought, chuckling to herself, Marco's sixteen, and I'm only thirteen. He'll probably lose interest in me really quickly. There might not even be a next time. A little ripple of fear ran through her. Maybe he had even forgotten about meeting her at Sand Dollar Beach today.

Her fears faded as she rounded a curve in the road. Out in the water, about a hundred feet offshore, was the rock. That had to be it. It was huge and long and looked as if it had dropped out of the sky and landed on one end. A motorcycle was parked off the road and a lone figure sat hunched on the beach looking out to sea. It was Marco.

Jana pulled her bike up next to his motorcycle and pushed down the kickstand. A narrow path led down to the water's edge. Jana took a deep breath of the salty air and plucked a blade of sea grass as she walked quietly toward him.

Marco seemed to be lost in thought and didn't notice her as she knelt behind him. Carefully, she touched the back of his ear with the tip of the blade of grass. He swatted it, but went on staring at the sea.

Jana touched him again, and he swatted his ear again. She put her hand over her mouth and tried to hold in a giggle, but couldn't. He whirled around.

"Why, you!" he said, leaping to his feet.

Jana jumped up and scurried out of his reach.

"You'll pay for that, wise guy," Marco said, laughing and running after her.

Jana ran along the shore as fast as she could, but it was only an instant before he caught her. The next thing she knew, he had picked her up and was carrying her to the water's edge, laughing like crazy.

"*One!*" he yelled, swinging her back and forth over the water.

"No! No!" Jana screamed.

"*Two!*" He swung her again.

"Mar-*co!*"

"And *three!*" He let her loose, and Jana went sailing out over the water.

She heard herself shriek as she fought to land on her feet. Instead, she landed on her back with a huge splash. She came up laughing, her hair plastered over her face.

Marco was next to her in a flash. "Are you okay?" he asked, grinning.

"You *rat!*" Jana cried, laughing and pushing her hair back out of her eyes. "Look at my shorts and top. I'll get you for this." She splashed water in his direction.

He ducked away. "I've got a towel in my saddlebags. I'll get it for you if you promise to be nice."

Jana stuck her tongue out at him.

Later, after she had dried her hair and as much of the rest of herself as possible, they sat on the beach in the warm sun.

"You were so out of it when I got here," said Jana. "What were you thinking about?"

"Nothing," he said. "Sometimes it's better not to think. When I come here, I try to just sit and let my island soak into my mind and my body."

Jana looked at Marco. He seemed so sensitive and deep.

"Let me show you something," Marco said suddenly, getting up and pulling Jana to her feet beside him.

Wading out into the water, he pointed to a sandbar not far away. "See that crescent beach? It's new. The currents in the Caribbean just formed it in the last couple of months. The tourists haven't found it yet."

He took her hand and waded through shallow water out to the sandbar.

When they reached it, Jana stopped suddenly. Along the sandbar's edge, the water was filled with hundreds of tiny starfish. "*Look! Look!*" she cried in amazement. The water was crystal clear, and there were starfish as far as she could see.

"I told you this was a special place," Marco said. "Look here, too."

Jana glanced where he was pointing, and her eyes opened wide in amazement. There were hundreds of round, flat shells of all sizes. In their centers were beautiful five-pointed designs.

"Sand dollars," said Marco. "That's why I call this place Sand Dollar Beach."

Jana sighed. "They're beautiful," she said, reaching down to pick one up. "The whole island is beautiful."

Marco smiled. "Barbados is a little different from where you come from, huh?"

"Yes, definitely a *lot* different."

"Well, you've got things where you come from that we don't have here."

"Like what?" she asked, turning the sand dollar so she could see its design better.

"Oh, you've got lots of big cities and all kinds of things happening."

"Right," she said, laughing. "And we've got pollution and snow and slush and crime and *too* many people. You're the one who has everything."

"Maybe," he said, smiling. "Here." He put a sand dollar on a thin gold chain into her hand and folded her fingers over it. "Something to remember me by. I made it into a necklace just for you."

Jana looked up into his dark eyes and felt as if she could swim in them.

His face brightened. "Enough of this seriousness,"

he said, taking her by the hand. "I can't stay long, so let's enjoy the time we have."

Jana nodded, squeezing the sand dollar he had given her tightly and falling into step beside him as they walked along the beach.

Melanie was sitting on a stone bench in the garden on the far side of the hotel from their villa at exactly two o'clock. It was very secluded and there were pathways and other benches where people could sit among the multi-colored, sweet-smelling flowers. The garden was empty. What a romantic place to meet Marco, she thought. Maybe the two of them would become famous secret lovers like Romeo and Juliet. A little shiver of excitement went up her spine.

When Marco arrived, he looked a little worn-out. His hair was a mess of dark curls, and his clothes were rumpled. He still looks totally gorgeous to me, thought Melanie.

"Hi," Marco said, grinning.

Melanie grinned back. It amazed her how easy it felt to be with him. Even though he was older than she was there was something so natural about being with him.

"Aren't you going to ask me to sit down?" he asked.

"Sure," she said, moving over to make room.

Marco reached up and plucked a large red flower from a bush and pushed it into Melanie's hair alongside her face. "There," he said, looking satisfied. "That completes the picture of a beautiful young lady sitting in a tropical garden. You know, it seems as if I've known you for a long time."

I knew it, Melanie told herself. *He feels the same way I do. It's true love.*

Together they sat talking quietly and looking at all the flowers in the garden.

A short time later Marco stood up.

"I've got to go," he said.

"Oh, no. Already?" asked Melanie, trying to hide her disappointment.

"I don't want to, but there's this guy I have to see." There was a trace of irritation in Marco's voice. "It's important. I'm not the one who's on vacation, you know."

Melanie looked at him, surprised at the change in tone. "It's just that we didn't have much time together."

"We'll see each other again," he said brightly.

"We will?" she said, cheering up. "When?"

"Soon," he said. "I've told Captain Smyth I'd help give scuba lessons in the morning, but I'll figure something out."

"Are you sure?" asked Melanie. "You're not just saying that?"

"Of course not," he said, taking her hand. "Trust me."

Melanie nodded. She couldn't wait to see him again!

Katie looked at her watch. It was ten after three. Had Marco forgotten he was supposed to meet her by the Jet Ski concession?

She shifted her feet in the sand and glanced around nervously. She looked at The Caribbean Sands hotel in the distance. What if one of her friends were to come along and see her standing there? She moved closer to the concession stand so she'd be less obvious, and the boy sitting inside looked at her curiously.

Her worries disappeared when she saw Marco emerge from some nearby palm trees. He was running toward her, and a feeling of elation filled her when she realized he was hurrying because of her.

"Sorry I'm late," said Marco, panting as he stopped in front of her. "This has been a busy day for me. I'm having a tough time making all my appointments."

"That's okay, I wasn't worried," Katie lied. "You must have a lot of people you have to see when you're in the music business."

"Something like that," answered Marco. "But now it's time for just *you* and *me*." The way he said it made Katie feel that she was really special.

Katie looked down the beach toward The Caribbean Sands hotel and froze.

"What's wrong?" asked Marco.

She squinted. "I think my friends are coming." In the distance Katie could see four figures who looked like Christie, Melanie, Jana, and Beth walking toward them. "What'll we do?"

Marco turned to the boy in the concession stand. "Hey, Lonnie. Can we use one of your Jet Skis?"

"Sure, Marco. Business is slow, anyway. Just remember me when I want to go scuba diving sometime."

"You got it," Marco said, and started pushing one of the Jet Skis into the water.

Katie looked at the four girls who were walking in their direction. Had they seen her and Marco yet? Did they recognize Katie? If they did, she would have to beg them not to breathe a word about the two of them being together. It could cost Marco his job.

"Come on," called Marco as the Jet Ski floated away.

Katie waded in after him and scrambled up onto the machine.

He jumped up behind her, reached over her shoulder, and pulled the starter cable. The motor wheezed but didn't catch.

Katie looked back at the girls on the beach. One of them was pointing toward them. Katie turned her face away quickly and tried to make herself disappear in Marco's shadow.

He pulled the starter again, and a plume of blue smoke belched out of the exhaust pipe as the motor burst into life. Marco twisted the throttle, and the Jet Ski jumped like a dolphin and then surged away from the beach.

A few moments later, Katie looked back over her shoulder. Now the girls looked like tiny specks. They had stopped at the concession stand and were talking to the boy who worked there. Were they questioning him because they recognized her? Katie wondered. She dreaded going back to the villa. If they had spotted her, she would have a lot of explaining to do about why she was with Marco and why she had kept her seeing him a secret.

Katie settled back against Marco's chest and tried to enjoy the wind on her face and the splashes of water as the Jet Ski jumped from wave to wave. Well, she thought, if The Fabulous Five did see me with Marco, there's nothing I can do about it now.

CHAPTER

"You guys are no fun at all," said Jeffy, looking as if he were about to cry.

"Find something to do by yourself, you little wart," said Melanie. "Go make a sand castle or something."

Melanie, Jana, Beth, and Christie were drinking sodas on the patio with Mr. and Mrs. Edwards.

"I don't *want* to make a sand castle," Jeffy protested. "Why don't you come down to the beach so I can bury you? Pleeeeese!" He grabbed Melanie's arm and started pulling. "Come on, Mel."

"I don't want to be buried," Melanie said. "I just want to be left alone."

"Larry, why don't you take Jeffy for a walk?" Mrs.

Edwards said to her husband. "Maybe you can find him a new beach toy."

"Or look up our cousin," Melanie offered.

"Didn't I tell you? I tried to find Milton Edwards, but he's not in the phone book," said her father. "I suppose that means he either moved . . . or died."

"That's too bad," said Melanie. "I guess you'll just have to find a new toy for Jeffy then."

Mr. Edwards shook his head sadly. "He's got every kind of beach toy there is. I don't know how we'll get them all home as it is. But come on, Jeffy. We'll find something to do. Maybe we can find a couple of Barbados babes who'd like to hook up with two good-looking dudes from the States."

Mrs. Edwards gave her husband a that'll-be-the-day look as the two got up to leave.

"Look. Here comes Katie," said Beth.

Katie was walking slowly up the beach with her head down. When she reached the patio, she glanced quickly around at the others.

"Did you get lost?" asked Christie. "It's almost five o'clock."

"What happened to your clothes?" asked Jana. "They're wet."

Katie let out a sigh of relief. Obviously her friends hadn't recognized her on the beach with Marco.

"I was just walking on the beach and a wave caught me by surprise," she explained hastily. "I'll go in and change before dinner."

"It sounds as if you girls are having a pretty good time," said Mrs. Edwards. "It's too bad there aren't more kids your age around."

"Oh, that's all right, Mrs. Edwards. I'm finding plenty of fun things to do," Christie said quickly.

"Me, too," chimed in Katie, who had just come back outside with dry clothing. "Marco and I . . ." She stopped in midsentence.

The others stared at her.

"Marco and you what?" asked Beth.

"I didn't mean Marco and me," Katie said, blushing. "I was going to say Marco and Tony. That's it. I think Marco and Tony look a lot alike."

"What's that got to do with having fun?" asked Christie looking bewildered.

Katie shrugged. "I just thought of it because I like the band."

"Well, I'm having the time of my life," interjected Melanie. "I just keep thinking about how jealous everyone back at home must be. Laura McCall's probably shoveling snow and eating her heart out, knowing we're here on a tropical island basking in the sun."

"Well, I did find out one thing that should interest

you," said Melanie's mother. "There's going to be a big New Year's Eve party here at The Caribbean Sands, complete with fireworks on the beach."

"You're kidding!" said Beth. "Fireworks on the beach? That sounds great. Can we go?"

"Of course," said Mrs. Edwards, chuckling. "It will be our last night on Barbados, and Mr. Edwards and I wouldn't want you to miss it for anything. Besides, that band you girls like so much will be playing for the party."

"Marco Montavo is singing? Super!" gushed Jana.

The others glanced at her, surprised at the outburst, and she sank down in her chair.

"Well, if you girls will excuse me, I think I'll shower and start getting ready for dinner," said Mrs. Edwards. "On the way to the dining room you can check the poster in the lobby to find out more about New Year's Eve."

"The New Year's Eve party sounds like fun," said Christie, poking at the ice in the bottom of her glass with a straw. "I'm glad *Marco* will be there with his band since it's our last night on the island."

"*Marco* really is a good singer," said Beth, glad that Christie had brought his name up again. She was absolutely dying to talk about him. "I wouldn't be surprised if he becomes a big star someday."

"Yeah," Jana said in a dreamy voice. "I can just see the concert advertisements. *Now appearing—in person—from the Caribbean island of Barbados—Marco Montavo!* We'd have to go see him, of course."

"Of course," said Melanie. "*Marco* would be hurt if we didn't."

Katie felt a twinge of anger as she listened to her friends go on about Marco. They were all talking as if he were their personal property. She was the one who had just spent time alone with him.

"I'm starting to get hungry," said Beth, abruptly changing the subject.

Christie nodded. "Me, too."

"Let's get dressed and go to the dining room," suggested Jana. "We have plenty of time to stop in the lobby and check the New Year's Eve party poster."

The girls made a mad dash for their rooms, and Melanie grabbed the shower first. As she massaged shampoo into her hair, she wondered how she'd keep her romance with Marco a secret. It wouldn't be easy—not after the way everyone had been talking about him on the patio. It was obvious they were all interested in him, and she needed to find a way to tell them that he liked her, without getting him in trouble at the hotel.

The five of them were dressed and ready for dinner

in record time. They stopped in the lobby and read the poster:

New Year's Eve
at the Caribbean Sands Village
Dinner and Dancing
Free Noisemakers and Hats
Fireworks on the Beach at Midnight
Make Your Reservations Early

"Wow!" said Melanie with a sigh. "This is going to be the best New Year's Eve ever!"

After dinner, The Fabulous Five wandered over to the dance floor and grabbed a table right in front of the bandstand.

When the band arrived a short while later, Marco flashed a smile at The Fabulous Five's table and then started setting up the band's equipment.

When everything was ready, Marco held the microphone to his lips. "Good evening, ladies and gentlemen, *chicos y chicas!*" and the air was filled with the ringing sounds of steel drums and the strumming of guitars as Marco sang the rhythmic Caribbean melody. The band followed with an even livelier song, and soon everyone was swaying and clapping to the music.

"Isn't Marco great?" said Jana when the band stopped for a break.

Christie looked at her critically. "Why are you talking about Marco so much all of a sudden?" she demanded. "Have you forgotten all about Randy?"

"Of . . . course not," Jana fumbled.

"So, why do you care, Christie?" asked Beth. "Unless, of course, *you* have a crush on Marco."

Christie felt her face turning red. "I was just asking. You're the one who said you thought he'd be a big star some day, Beth. Maybe *you've* got a crush on him."

"Just because I said he's a good singer doesn't mean I've got a crush on him. There are lots of good male singers, but I don't like them all."

"You've all been acting kind of funny," said Katie.

"*We* have?" asked Melanie. "What about you? You've never been interested in taking walks by yourself before. Where do you go anyway, Katie?"

Katie was sorry she had spoken up. "I told you. I've just been going for walks on the beach. I'm not the only one who goes off by herself. Beth goes shopping and Christie plays tennis. And you, Jana, you left by yourself after lunch."

"Wait a minute," said Jana. "We're here to have fun, not argue. Why's everyone getting so upset?"

The Fabulous Five stared at each other uneasily.

Just then Marco stepped up on the stage. Pulling the

hand mike off its stand, he moved closer to the audience. "Ladies and gentlemen, are there any new arrivals to our wonderful island of Barbados?"

Three couples raised their hands.

"Where are you from?" Marco asked, approaching another table.

"California!" yelled a middle-aged man and woman.

"Let's hear it for California!" shouted Marco, clapping his hands. The Fabulous Five applauded with the rest of the crowd.

"Illinois!" shouted a young man who was with a young woman.

"Is this your honeymoon?" asked Marco.

"That's right," the man answered.

"Let's hear it for the honeymooners!" called Marco, and the applause was even louder than before.

"And you, sir and madam?" Marco asked, pointing to the third couple.

The man stood up and threw both fists into the air. "Texas!" he shouted.

Part of the crowd cheered and the other part booed. The man laughed good-naturedly and sat down.

Marco's good looks and smile were obviously winning over the crowd. The Fabulous Five were mesmerized as he moved easily across the dance floor.

"And now I'd like to introduce some people who are

really special," continued Marco. "In fact, they're *fabulous*!" He signaled the band with one hand, and they started playing a cha-cha. "Ladies and gentlemen . . . *The Fabulous Five*!"

The girls froze, their mouths open and their eyes as big as saucers.

Marco danced over to their table and took Beth by the hand and pulled her out onto the stage. The other four stared in disbelief as he danced with her. Beth looked up at him with a mixture of awe and adoration.

Suddenly, he left Beth standing and took Jana's hand and led her out onto the stage. The audience started clapping in time to the music again as the two of them did some quick cha-cha steps. Next he approached Katie, then Melanie, and finally Christie. After he had all five of the girls onstage, he put them in a circle and they all danced together. The clapping grew louder.

Marco signaled the band again and the music changed to "De Congaline." The Fabulous Five fell in step behind him, laughing as they danced their way though the tables, adding dancers to the line as they went. Soon, everyone was dancing and clapping, the way they had the night before.

When the evening ended, the girls walked slowly back to the villa.

"I'm not sleepy yet," said Christie as they reached

the door. "I think I'll sit on the beach for a while and look at the stars."

The others said good-night and went inside. Christie pulled off her shoes and dropped down on the sand near the water.

She picked up a shell and wrote MARCO + CHRISTIE in the damp sand. Then she reached forward and scooped up a shellfull of water, filling in the lines so that the words she had drawn in the sand gleamed like liquid silver in the moonlight.

She had forgotten about the terrible game of tennis she had played and remembered only her walk afterward with Marco. Her happiness was clouded only by a small, niggling irritation at her four best friends for paying so much attention to Marco lately. Why had they gotten so upset tonight when they were talking about him? Did they have crushes on him, too?

Beth felt miserable as she tossed and turned in her bed. What was going on with her friends, anyway? They had intentionally made her sit where she couldn't see Marco and the band last night. What was worse, he couldn't see her. Of course, tonight he had chosen her first to dance the cha-cha with him. That had to mean something. And yet . . . her friends all seemed to be interested in him, too. How could she let them know that she was the one he liked? She was bursting to shout it out loud. I guess I can't, she thought, not without betraying his confidence.

Jana lay quietly on her side. She was holding the sand-dollar necklace Marco had given her at the beach. What a day! It had been so much fun with him chasing her along the water and then throwing her in. He liked her, she knew he did. But what about Randy? It had startled her when Christie reminded her of her boyfriend back home. And why had Christie brought Randy's name up anyway? Could she tell that Marco liked Jana? Was Christie jealous? It wasn't Jana's fault that Marco liked her. It was just her good luck.

Wow! My flirting tips *really* worked this time, thought Melanie as she lay in the dark. Marco likes me. I've got to remember *exactly* how I did each and every one of the tips. I could be *awesome* if I get it down perfect. She stuffed the corner of the bed sheet in her mouth to keep from giggling at the thought.

A small feeling of depression came over her as she remembered a few things about the evening that hadn't been quite perfect, such as the argument they'd all had. I suppose Marco *had* to choose someone else to dance with first so no one would suspect he likes me, she tried to reassure herself. But why did Katie have to be right beside him? And why were there stars in Jana's eyes every time she looked at him?

Katie let out a deep sigh as she thought about the wonderful time she'd had with Marco that afternoon. He made her feel all tingly inside. One part of her was relieved her friends hadn't seen them together on the beach, but another part of her wanted them to know her secret. It was hard keeping such big news from her best friends in the whole world.

Katie frowned in the darkness. Would the rest of The Fabulous Five be glad about the time I've been spending with Marco? she wondered. Maybe it was her imagination, but after tonight she couldn't help thinking that they really did have crushes on Marco. Katie had seen Beth's face when the singer pulled her up to dance, and even Christie, who was usually too busy for boys, seemed totally entranced by Marco on the dance floor.

And Jana and Melanie had acted just as lovesick every time the singer came near. They would all be so embarrassed if they found out that Marco likes me, Katie thought. I don't want that to happen. It wasn't fair to keep her relationship with Marco a secret from her best friends, but on the other hand, maybe it was best they didn't know the truth.

CHAPTER

10

"You're back early," Mr. Edwards said as Christie came into the villa carrying her tennis racket the next morning. Melanie's parents were still finishing their coffee.

"I couldn't find a partner," Christie replied in a dejected tone.

"Well, join the crowd of gloomies," he said, indicating Melanie, Jana, Beth, and Katie, who were sitting on the patio looking depressed.

"Things sure have fallen apart since yesterday when I complimented them for being so chipper," said Mrs. Edwards, shaking her head. "You wouldn't believe it's

114

the same group of girls." Turning back to them, she asked, "Why don't you go swimming?"

She was answered by five sets of shrugging shoulders.

Mr. Edwards took a sip of his coffee. "I read on the bulletin board in the lobby that Captain Smyth is taking a group to Folkestone Underwater Park this morning to dive around an old sunken ship. You girls took scuba lessons. Had you thought about going along?"

The Fabulous Five all jerked upright in their chairs.

"Did it say if he was the only instructor who will be there?" asked Melanie eagerly.

"No, but there was a sign-up sheet next to it with a lot of names on it. I'd think he'd need help with a group that size," responded her father.

"I think I'll go," said Christie, getting up quickly.

"Me, too," said Beth, heading for her bedroom.

Melanie was right behind them, and Jana and Katie made a dash for their room, too. They reappeared almost instantly dressed in swimsuits. "See you later," called Melanie as they rushed out the door.

"Well, now," Captain Smyth said, frowning at the small spiral notebook he held in his hand. "I don't see any of your names on the list. Do we have enough air tanks for these five girls, Marco?"

Marco nodded, not looking at any of them.

"Okay, we'll find room for you, somehow. Listen up, everybody," the captain announced to the people waiting for his instructions. "We'll be going to Folkestone Underwater Park this morning, which is about ten miles up the coast on the other side of Bridgetown. Folkestone is a marine reserve, which means it's a conservation area for undersea life. There are a lot of things for us to see there, like *Stavronika*, which is a sunken freighter. There are also coral reefs and just about any undersea life you can think of. The people who run the place are very particular about how you treat things in the park, so don't break off coral, harass the moray eels, or anything like that."

Soft laughter rippled through the crowd, and the girls exchanged excited grins.

"Now . . . we've got two vans out front," the captain went on. "Take your things and find a seat in one of them. We'll be a wee bit crowded, but we'll make do."

The Fabulous Five were the first ones out the front of the hotel. When Marco headed for the second van and got behind the wheel, the five girls rushed for it, too. Melanie, Beth, and Jana got to the front seat next to Marco first. Christie and Katie shot frowns at their friends and grudgingly got into the bench seat behind them.

"Could I have a little room, please?" asked Marco, who was pushed up against the driver's door because there were four people in the front seat.

Melanie smiled apologetically and scooted toward Beth, but she could hardly contain her excitement over getting to sit next to him. She purposely did not look at any of her friends as they made the trip to Folkestone in silence.

When they arrived at the parking lot, everyone piled out, and Captain Smyth and Marco distributed diving tanks and masks to everyone. Then they all marched down to a dock, where they boarded a small boat and headed out to sea.

"Okay, everyone," said Captain Smyth when they had reached the diving area. "This is a good place to start. It's relatively shallow here, and there's a lot to see. Marco and I will take you in one at a time and get you started. When you feel comfortable being by yourself, we leave you alone. Now you all remember the signal if you need help, don't you?"

Everyone nodded.

"Good. Both Marco and I'll be swimming around down there, too, so just look for one of us if you need anything."

Melanie eased herself toward the side of the boat where Marco and Captain Smyth were helping the tourists put on their equipment.

"As soon as your tanks are on, jump into the water and clean your masks," called out Marco. "Then raise your hand, and either the captain or I will start you diving."

Melanie strapped on her tank and grabbed her mask. She wanted to get into the water before Marco got distracted by someone else.

"Last one in is a rotten egg," shouted Katie as she streaked past Melanie and hit the water with a splash.

Melanie clenched her fists and watched in anger as Katie hurriedly cleaned her mask and then swam up beside Marco and raised her hand to signal she was ready to dive.

Katie thought Marco looked strangely uneasy as he acknowledged her signal and reached for her hand. Was it because there were so many people around, and he was afraid that someone would notice them together and guess they liked each other? Probably, she assured herself. After all, he couldn't be too careful.

Once they were underwater, Marco seemed to relax. He grinned at her, sending plumes of bubbles up each side of his face. She couldn't help laughing. He looked so funny with his long hair floating up toward the surface of the water like long strands of seaweed.

They swam side by side through the indigo-blue water, and Katie was almost sorry when they reached a beautiful ledge of coral. Marco pointed to the formations and to the silvery fish peeking shyly out at them from crevices in the rock. Then he gave her a questioning look, asking if she would be okay if he left her now. She had to nod. He had other divers to help. He nodded back and waved as he floated back toward the surface.

Melanie was watching when Marco's head bobbed above the water. Her jealousy disappeared when she saw Katie wasn't with him. Melanie had cleaned her mask about a dozen times while she waited for him to surface.

She pushed back her bangs and slipped the mask over her face. Just then someone grabbed her arm. Startled, she whirled around in the water and came face-to-face with a beaming Captain Smyth.

"Aha! Another creature is ready to descend into the deep blue sea," he said gleefully.

Out of the corner of her eye, Melanie could see Christie tapping Marco on the shoulder. "Rats!" she muttered under her breath. But there was nothing to do but dive with Captain Smyth and look for Marco when she got underwater.

The descent was easier than Melanie had expected, and in no time she felt confident enough to be left on her own. The captain gave her a snappy salute and pushed off for the surface again, leaving her close to a tall mound of coral.

Melanie looked around at the brightly colored fish swimming near her. Lots of other divers were nearby, poking among the reefs and chasing after the fish. Melanie was instantly fascinated by the underwater scenery. There were orange fish and yellow fish and fish with vertical black stripes. There were many different kinds of coral, too. Some looked like layers of mushrooms, some looked like huge gnarled brains, and some like tall, delicate castles. She was so entranced by it all that for a few moments she forgot to look for Marco.

Then she spotted him again. This time he was with Beth. Her jealousy returned as she watched the two of them glide through the water like a pair of synchronized swimmers.

Melanie treaded in place for a moment and watched them. They seemed to be having a wonderful time. *Too* wonderful a time, she decided.

Slowly Melanie circled around until she was behind them and hid in back of a tall piece of coral where she could watch without being seen.

They were too far away to see clearly. Melanie rubbed the surface of her mask, but it didn't help. What were they doing now?

She squinted through the murky water. *If Beth was flirting with Marco, she would never speak to her again!* They were supposed to be friends.

Just then Marco reached out and put his hands on Beth's shoulders.

"Whaaaaat!" Melanie started to cry, but the sound ended in a blast of bubbles as her breathing hose burst out of her mouth.

Melanie started to panic, clamping her hand over her mouth so that she wouldn't gulp water. She wanted to breathe through her nose, but she knew she couldn't. Thrashing around, she tried to grab her breathing hose and hold her breath at the same time, but her movement and the pressure of the oxygen coming out of the hose sent it flailing around furiously in the water, just out of her grasp.

The signal! she thought. What was the signal? She couldn't remember. There were too many bubbles swirling in the water around her to see Marco or anyone else or to know if anyone could see her.

Suddenly strong arms wrapped around her, and she could make out Marco's face near hers. He was trying to calm her, to tell her to continue holding her breath, but her lungs were on fire. She thought she was going to explode.

An instant later Marco gently pushed the breathing hose back into her mouth, reassuring her calmly with his gestures. Slowly she inhaled. Oxygen filled her lungs, and she exhaled through her nose.

Melanie was dizzy with relief. Putting her head on Marco's shoulder, she breathed in and out while her heartbeat slowed to normal. Then Marco took her by the hand and pulled her slowly toward the surface.

Melanie decided not to go back into the water after her disastrous experience with the breathing hose, so she spent the rest of the afternoon sunbathing on the deck while the others continued to dive. She was still angry at Beth for flirting with Marco, but she vowed never to admit to anyone what had really happened underwater.

After they had explored the reefs for an hour or so, the captain started up the boat's engine and took them out to the site where the *Stavronika* was lying in the sand on the bottom. After additional words of caution about not trying to go inside the old freighter, he let them go overboard and dive on their own.

This time Marco swam with Christie, pointing out the thick layer of barnacles that covered the hull and laughing with her when a school of tiny fish came darting out through a porthole. Christie forgot her anger at her friends until Jana appeared above them, frog-kicking through the water and motioning for them to follow her.

Christie shook her head vigorously. She didn't care what great underwater discovery Jana had made, she wasn't about to follow. She had Marco all to herself, and she didn't like Jana's butting in.

Suddenly Jana dove down beside them. She was pointing eagerly and tugging on Marco's hand. She hardly even looked at Christie.

Marco shrugged, giving Christie an apologetic grin, and swam off with Jana. Christie watched them go, and in spite of the coolness of the water, she could feel her blood begin to boil.

The Fabulous Five made the trip back to shore in silence. Melanie was still embarrassed over losing her breathing hose and angry at Beth. Christie and Jana ignored each other and sat staring over opposite sides of the boat at the water as it churned by. Katie kept a suspicious eye on Melanie, and Beth sat quietly by herself.

To make matters worse, Marco ignored them and took care of the scuba gear. When they reached shore, they marched solemnly up the pier.

As the tourists waited by the vans for Captain Smyth to return, Marco sat on a bench by himself writing in the captain's notebook. When he was finished, he tore the pages out, folded them separately, and then stood up and whistled to himself. He flashed a smile at The Fabulous Five, and each of them wondered if it had been meant for her, or for one of her friends.

"Well, how did it go?" asked Mr. Edwards as the girls trooped back into the villa later.

"Fine," said Melanie over her shoulder as she dashed into one of the bedrooms and closed the door behind her.

Christie zipped into the bathroom just in front of Beth, who stamped her foot in anger and then made for the other bathroom.

Katie went into the other bedroom before Jana could reach it. Jana spun around and went out onto the patio.

Christie unfolded the paper Marco had sneaked into her hand as he helped her get into the van and spread it out on the lavatory. It said:

Rent a bike and meet me at Sand Dollar Beach tomorrow at eight in the morning. It's a special place. Here's how you get there.

Underneath was a map, which looked easy to follow.

A thrill went up Christie's back. She had been wrong to be upset with Jana. Marco wanted to see her.

While Christie was reading her note in one bathroom, Beth was doing the same thing in the other bathroom. The words and the map on Beth's note were identical to the one's on Christie's except for the time, which was ten A.M. "I was foolish to worry about Melanie," Beth mumbled to herself. "Marco was only trying to help her."

She folded the note and gazed toward the ceiling. She had liked meeting Marco at The Flying Fish, but meeting him at a lonely spot on the beach seemed even more romantic.

Jana's note didn't include a map, since she already knew where Sand Dollar Beach was. Marco wanted her to meet him there at noon. Jana moved to sit on the wall at the edge of the patio and looked out at the ocean. A smile crept over her face as she thought about the secret place she and Marco were going to meet at again. So what if he had spent time underwater with Christie? It was his job.

Melanie lay on her stomach on the bed and punched her fists into the pillows. "Hooray," she whispered. *"He wants to see me! He wants to see me!"* She rolled over and looked at the note again.

"Tomorrow at two o'clock and there's even a map. How romantic can you *get*?" she said aloud. "And I was worried that he didn't like me anymore. How could I have doubted?"

Katie sat on the edge of the bed in her bedroom and held her note tightly in both hands. A rendezvous on the beach at four tomorrow. That sounded so perfect.

It was fun riding the Jet Ski with Marco, but they couldn't really talk on one because of the noise, and he was always seated in back of her. She couldn't wait to meet him at the beach and have a serious discussion with him. She really wanted to find out more about him and what he thought about things such as women's rights. Well . . . tomorrow she would have him all to herself.

CHAPTER

11

"*H*ello!" Christie called as she parked her bicycle at the edge of the road near Marco's motorcycle. Sand Dollar Beach had been easy to find with the big rock sticking out of the water. And it had been pretty easy to leave the villa this morning without the rest of The Fabulous Five asking questions. Although everyone had seemed more cheerful by dinnertime last night, there was still some tension in the air.

Marco waved at her.

"What a beautiful place," exclaimed Christie, surveying the white sand that stretched in both directions. She kicked off her sandals and tested the water. "It's so warm," she said. "You're lucky you have the Caribbean to swim in any time you want."

Marco smiled and took her hand and they started wading in the shallow water along the shore.

"I bet you've got lots of places to swim in the States," Marco said.

"Mostly swimming pools. At the Y or city pool, and they're full of chlorine." Changing the subject, she said, "I noticed the band was off last night. I'm glad you weren't the one sick."

Marco nodded. "Me too. I was glad to have a night off."

"What do you do on your night off? There must be things to do on Barbados that tourists don't know about."

Marco laughed. "Not really."

"Come on," said Christie. "You can't tell me that you don't have hangouts tourists don't know about."

He looked at her sharply. "Where would they be? There are only so many places you can go to on an island, and I've been to all of them a million times. This is not like the United States, you know. We don't have thousands and thousands of square miles of country. You ought to try living on an island all your life. You might not think it's so special."

"But you've got all these beautiful beaches and palm

trees, and the weather is so fantastic all year round," protested Christie.

"Like Magnum, P.I., says on television: 'Another boring day in paradise,'" responded Marco. "Everything we do on Barbados has to do with people who come here from someplace else."

"Oh," Christie said quietly, looking up into Marco's serious eyes.

A sparkling smile lit his face. "Let me show you something," he said, leading her out to a small sandbar. "This is why I call it Sand Dollar Beach."

Christie looked down into the water. "Oh! They're beautiful," she said, reaching down and picking up a sand dollar. The star-shaped design on the top of the shell was prettier than any she had ever seen on a sand dollar. "And there are hundreds of them."

"And look over here," he said, pointing.

"Wow!" Christie exclaimed at the sight of thousands of tiny starfish.

"See why I wanted you to meet me here?" he asked. "It's a special place and I wouldn't show it to anyone but you."

Christie looked up at him and smiled. "This is our place?" she asked.

"Yes, that's right. Just yours and mine," he answered.

They walked through the water together looking at

all the underwater life until Marco looked at his watch
and said, "I hate to say it, but I've got to go."

Christie made a face to show her disappointment.

"But I've got something I made for you," he said.
"Hold out your hand and close your eyes."

Christie did as she was told. When she opened her
eyes, she found he had put a sand dollar on a chain in
her hand.

"It's beautiful," she said as she started to put the
chain over her head.

Marco stopped her. "Could you not wear it now?"
he asked. "Maybe you could keep it a secret until you
get home. Someone might ask you where you got it,
and I wouldn't want you lying for me."

Christie smiled at him. He was so sweet. "Okay,"
she said, and put it in her shorts pocket.

Beth stopped her bike at the curve in the road next to
the motorcycle. There was the big rock Marco had put
in the drawing he had given her. She looked at her
watch. It was ten A.M. exactly. Where was Marco?

"Hi."

Beth jumped, whirling around to find him standing
behind her.

"Sorry," he said, laughing. "I didn't mean to scare

you. I thought I saw an eagle's nest on that cliff on the other side of the road and I went to check it out. No such luck, though."

"Park your bike," he added. "I want to show you something in the water."

An hour later, Beth and Marco walked back up to the road hand in hand.

"This sand-dollar necklace you made for me is beautiful, Marco," said Beth, squeezing his hand. "And I *will* keep it a secret. But whenever I think of you, I'll reach into my pocket and touch it."

Beth climbed onto her bike and headed back in the direction of the hotel. As she reached the curve in the road, she glanced back over her shoulder for one more look at Marco. He gave her a big smile as he returned her last wave good-bye.

After Beth disappeared around the curve, Marco walked over to his motorcycle and opened one of the saddlebags. Reaching in, he pulled out two more sand-dollar necklaces. Since he had given one to Jana the other day, and Christie and Beth each one this morning, these would be for Melanie and Katie.

He put one of the necklaces back in the saddlebag and scraped at the store label on the back of the other one with his thumbnail until he had it off. Then he polished the sand dollar against his shirt.

Marco looked at his watch. He had close to a half hour before Jana would be there. That would be enough time to take a swim. He stuck the sand-dollar necklace in his pocket and headed back down to the beach.

CHAPTER

12

Jana walked the bike up to the bicycle rental shop after she returned from her secret meeting with Marco.

"Oh, Jana. Hi."

Startled, Jana stopped in her tracks and looked up. Melanie, who looked equally surprised, was handing money to the man behind the counter.

"Er . . . uh, hi," responded Jana. Before Melanie could ask her where she had been, Jana said, "Where are you going?"

"I thought I would just, uh . . . you know, take a little ride," Melanie answered. "Where have you been?"

"Oh, er, uh . . . just riding, too. Where is everyone else?"

"Christie and Beth are lying out on the beach, and the last time I saw Katie, she was in her room brushing her hair," answered Melanie.

Jana noticed that Melanie was wearing eye makeup, which seemed strange when she was only going for a bike ride. Then she remembered her own makeup and quickly put her hand up as if she were shielding her eyes from the sun.

"Well, I'd better get moving if I'm going to be back in time for dinner," said Melanie, looking at her watch. She hopped on the bike and started pedaling down the street in the direction Jana had come from.

Jana looked after Melanie, who glanced back quickly over her shoulder one time before she disappeared around a street corner.

A while later, after she had left Marco at Sand Dollar Beach, Melanie was riding with no hands on her bicycle toward the hotel. Every once in a while, when there was no one around to hear, she would throw her arms up in the air and shout:

"*He likes me! Marco Montavo likes me!*"

Melanie took the sand-dollar necklace Marco had just given her out of her pocket and looked at it. It was so special. Marco had made it himself, and she would keep it forever.

A sixteen-year-old boy likes me, she thought exuberantly. This is the best vacation I've ever had. She stuffed the sand dollar back in her pocket, trying to turn a corner at the same time. But the handlebars on her bike swerved wildly and before she could straighten them out, the bike slammed into another bicycle that was coming around the corner at the same time.

"Melanie!" cried Katie. "*What are you doing?*" She picked herself up off the ground and brushed off her legs.

Melanie looked up wide-eyed from where she was sprawled in the grass. "I was riding a bike," she said weakly.

"I know that!" said Katie, examining a scrape on one knee.

"I'm sorry," said Melanie, jumping up and digging a tissue out of her pocket. "Here, let me help."

"What were you doing riding no hands, anyway?" asked Katie as Melanie wiped the blood off Katie's leg.

Melanie shrugged. "Just having fun. There. That's better," she said, looking at the wound.

"But look at my shorts," said Katie. "The whole side is dirty."

"Come on back to the villa and I'll get you a pair of my shorts."

"Oh, no! That's all right," Katie said quickly.

"But it will only take a minute," said Melanie.

Katie glanced nervously at her watch. "No," she said, "it's all right. I have to be . . . I mean, I'm just going for a bicycle ride anyway. It's no big deal." She gave Melanie a big smile.

"Well, if you say so," said Melanie uncertainly. "See you later." She watched Katie get on her bike and start off toward Sand Dollar Beach.

Melanie frowned.

Katie's sure not acting like herself today, she thought.

CHAPTER

13

*B*eth picked the red flower from the bush and held it to her nose. It smells fantastic, she thought. As a matter of fact, everything about Barbados is fantastic. Especially, one island boy named Marco Montavo. She clipped the flower in her hair with her barrette. It was Sunday, and Beth was on her way back to the hotel after spending time with Marco.

Thinking about Marco made Beth sad. Their vacation would be over on Tuesday and she would have to leave for home. What a way to spend New Year's Day, she thought. Her eyes filled with tears. Well, my New Year's resolution will be to see Marco again, she told herself, pushing her chin out stubbornly. She would write to him every week in care of The Caribbean Sands hotel. *No!* She would write to him *every day.* That would show him how much she cared for him. Maybe . . . just maybe, she could save enough money over the next year to come to Barbados again. She could baby-sit and wash cars and do all kinds of things to earn money. Besides, she'd be fourteen then, maybe her parents would let her come again. Or better still, maybe Melanie's father could win another vacation trip to Barbados.

Suddenly, Beth was aware of another bicyclist coming up the road. It was Jana. Beth waved, and Jana pulled over and stopped.

"Hi," said Jana. "What are doing way out here?"

"Picking flowers." Beth laughed, pointing to the one on her hair. "Isn't it beautiful?"

Jana nodded. "Is that your private bush or can I have one, too?"

"Feel free," said Beth. She followed Jana back to the bush.

"They're all so pretty, I don't know which one to choose," said Jana.

"There's a nice one down there," Beth said, pointing to a large blossom growing just above the ground.

As Jana bent to pick the flower, something fell out of her shorts pocket.

"You dropped this," said Beth, picking the object up. She froze when she saw what she had in her hand. It was a sand dollar with a delicate gold chain running through a hole at the top. It looked so much like the one Marco had given her, she automatically put her hand against her own pocket to see if hers was still there. It was.

Jana blushed a bright red and quickly took the necklace from Beth and stuck it back into her pocket. "Thanks," she said in a small voice.

Jana fumbled as she tried to poke the stem of the flower she had picked behind her ear. "Does that look okay?" she asked.

"Just a little bit more this way," said Beth, adjusting it for her. "Jana?"

"Yes?"

"Uh . . . nothing," responded Beth. "Never mind."

"I'd better get going," said Jana, "or I'll use up all my bicycle time without riding. Thanks for showing me the flowers, Beth. They're really neat."

Beth seemed lost in her own thoughts as Jana rode away.

That evening, after they had eaten dinner and watched Marco and the band perform one more time, The

Faublous Five were walking along the beach toward their villa. The silver moon lit the white sands, and the black water rolled quietly up onto the shore, ending in a frothy foam.

"Barbados is so beautiful," said Katie. "It's going to be hard to leave on Tuesday."

"I can't bear the thought of going back to school," said Melanie. "Think about it: math, history, English, Family Living classes. Yuck! If we were meant to live that way, why were beaches and palm trees invented?"

Jana laughed. "I agree. I don't want to think about having to leave all this."

"But don't forget, Randy and Scott and Tony and Keith and Jon are waiting at home," said Beth.

A silence fell over the group and the other girls looked in different directions, embarrassed by Beth's reminder of the boyfriends they had forgotten.

Beth looked at her friends and pulled something out of her pocket. It was her sand-dollar necklace. As she walked along, she put it around her neck.

Jana and Katie noticed what she was doing. They stopped and looked at her curiously.

Katie frowned. "That's pretty," she said, examining the necklace closely. "Where did you get it?"

"Oh, someone gave it to me," Beth said casually.

The others gathered around, looking closely at the sand-dollar necklace.

Jana bit her lower lip. "*Who* gave it to you?"

Beth looked from Christie to Melanie to Jana to Katie as they stared at her, waiting for her answer. From the looks on their faces, what she had suspected, when she saw the necklace fall out of Jana's pocket was true. Well, she thought, taking in a deep breath, we might as well get it out in the open. "Marco gave it to me."

"*Marco?*" cried Christie.

"That's right," answered Beth. "He said he made it for me."

No one spoke for a moment. Then Jana reached into her pocket and pulled out her sand-dollar necklace, holding it up by the chain so the others could see. "He said he made *this one* for *me*."

Slowly, Melanie, Katie, and Christie pulled out their sand dollars, and the five of them stood in a circle holding up their identical necklaces in stunned silence.

Jana was the first to speak. "Wow. He really made fools of us, didn't he?" she said in a soft voice.

"Really," answered Katie. "Just think how he's probably laughing at us right now for acting like lovesick little kids and being so naive. I've never been so embarrassed in my life."

Beth crossed her arms defiantly across her chest. "How gullible could we get?"

"Doesn't he have any feelings?" said Christie. "I mean, this hurts!"

Melanie nodded and brushed away a tear. The pain in her heart was too intense for her to speak. Ha! she thought to herself. Big-deal Melanie and her big-deal flirting tips just got taken for a ride.

"And to think," whispered Christie, "I was jealous of you guys. I even got mad every time I saw you talking to him. I blamed *you* when it was Marco who was the villain!"

Katie nodded. "Me, too. I was so mad at all of you that I couldn't think straight. What a jerk! He could have broken up The Fabulous Five."

"Well," said Jana sarcastically, "Marco must have a shop with a lot of elves making necklaces out of sand dollars so he can give them away to tourists."

"At least to *female* tourists," agreed Christie.

"Where . . . where did he give you the necklace?" asked Katie. She was afraid she already knew the answer to her question.

"Sand Dollar Beach," said Beth.

"Sand Dollar Beach," said Jana.

"The same place," said Melanie.

"Yup," said Christie.

"I still can't believe it," murmured Jana. "I thought he was so sincere."

"And I thought he was a sensitive person," said Christie.

"We all obviously thought he was a lot of things he isn't," said Beth.

"You have to admit he was pretty smart," added Katie.

Nobody said anything for a minute.

Finally Jana broke the silence. *"Oo-kaay, Fabulous Five!"* she said loudly, anger glinting in her eyes. "We can't let him get away with this. What are we going to do?"

"How about sticking his head in a steel drum and beating on it?" asked Melanie.

"Why don't we put laughing gas in his scuba tank so he can't stop laughing when he gets underwater?" muttered Katie. "It would serve him right after the way he's been laughing at us."

"Wait a minute, guys," said Jana. "Let's get serious and think of something that would really pay him back. Something he *deserves*."

There were murmurs and nods of agreement as they all began to think.

Again, it was Jana who spoke first. "What do you guys think about this?"

The rest of The Fabulous Five gathered in close as Jana started to tell them about her plan.

CHAPTER

$\mathcal{M}$arco was waiting at Sand Dollar Beach the next morning when Christie got there. She waved as she ran down the path to him.

"Wha . . . ?" he exclaimed as she threw herself against him and wrapped her arms around his waist.

"I missed you!" she said brightly, looking up into his eyes.

"We just saw each other last night," he protested.

"I know, but I *missed* you anyway," said Christie snuggling close to him and putting her cheek on his chest.

Marco untangled her arms from around himself. He looked embarrassed. "Hey, don't be this way. You know that you're going back to the States tomorrow. You'll see all your friends and tell them what a great time you had in Barbados. You'll forget all about me."

"No, I won't!"

"Sure you will," said Marco. "That's the way it is with tourists. You just think you like me."

"That's not true!" Christie protested. "And to prove it, I'm not going home!"

Marco's face went white. "You're *what*?"

"I'm not going home," repeated Christie. "I'm going to stay here with you." She had to bite her lip to keep from laughing at the horrified look on his face. Her story hit him just the way The Fabulous Five had known it would.

"Your parents would *never* let you do that," he said, shaking his head.

Christie put a determined look on her face. "They *couldn't* do anything about it if I ran away and hid. You know everything about Barbados. You could find a place to hide me. And we could be together." She threw her arms around him again.

"Wait a minute! I'm not going to help you run away," he growled, as he disentangled himself from her.

"Okay," Christie said, folding her arms. "If you won't help me, I'll find a way to do it myself."

"Don't do anything foolish," Marco begged. "Think about your parents. It would hurt them."

"I'll write them later," said Christie.

"Go on back to the hotel," Marco commanded. "I should have known better than to meet secretly with you in the first place," he said, pounding the sides of his head with his fists. "And what's more, I can't see you anymore. That's final."

A tear trickled down Christie's cheek. She sniffled and brushed it away. I ought to get an Academy Award for this, she thought. Beth would be proud of me. Christie turned on her heel and charged back up the slope.

"*You'll be sorry!*" she shouted over her shoulder.

"Hi," Beth said sweetly as she joined Marco on the beach a short while later. Beth had met Christie at the bicycle rental shop and had heard about the snow job she had done on Marco. The rest of The Fabulous Five were anxiously awaiting their turns at making him sweat.

"Hi," said Marco a little absent-mindedly.

"It's a *gorgeous* day," said Beth, facing the ocean and running a hand through her spiked hair.

"Yeah," said Marco.

Beth spun around and gave him her biggest smile. "I've made a decision."

He looked at her suspiciously. "What kind of decision?"

Beth couldn't resist teasing him. "I've decided to . . . buy a new outfit."

Relief washed over his face.

"And then I'm going to run away so Mr. and Mrs. Edwards can't make me go back home with them," she added quickly.

"*Hey, wait a minute!* Not you . . . !" He stopped short of finishing the sentence.

"Not me, what?" asked Beth.

"Nothing," said Marco, wiping off the perspiration that had suddenly popped out on his forehead. "Look. You can't run away. Your parents would be sick with worry. You'd end up being sent home anyway, so it doesn't make sense."

"Maybe it doesn't make sense to you," said Beth in a pouty tone, "but it does to me. I've always wanted to sing—you can add me to your act, couldn't you? We could sing love songs *together*! Just think how romantic that would be."

"That's a crazy idea," Marco muttered, sighing deeply.

Beth resisted a chuckle. For once Marco looked totally defeated. She almost felt sorry for him, until she re-membered what fools he had made of her and her friends.

"No matter what you say, I'm going to do it," she said. "If you won't let me sing with your band, I'll find another band on the island. We could still be together."

"I'll tell Mr. and Mrs. Edwards," Marco threatened.

"No, you won't," countered Beth. "Then everyone would know that you were having secret meetings with a girl who was staying at the hotel. You'd lose your job and probably wouldn't be able to get another one sing-ing at any hotel." She patted him on the arm soothingly. "Don't worry. It'll work out." He had a look in his eyes like a sick puppy.

"Well," Beth said cheerfully, "I've got some things to do, so I'll see you later. Remember, I'm counting on you not to tell anyone. Bye!"

When Jana reached the beach, Marco was sitting slumped dejectedly at the water's edge.

"What's wrong?" she asked, sitting down next to him. "You look sad."

When he looked up, Jana could see that everything Christie and Beth had said about their meetings with him that morning had been true. The look in his eyes

almost made her feel sorry for him. No! she told herself. He's a rat and deserves what we're doing to him.
How could I ever have thought he was sincere? He's
nothing like Randy.

"I just found out that an aunt of mine is ill," he said.

Jana put her hand up to her mouth to hide a smile.
She knew Marco was lying. He was really depressed
about Christie's and Beth's telling him they were going
to run away so they could be with him. He had been
happy when Christie first saw him that morning, and
he hadn't told either Christie or Beth about any aunt's
being sick.

"Oh, that's too bad," said Jana with all the make-
believe sympathy she could muster. "I'm so sorry."

He looked at her appreciatively. "I knew you'd
understand. You're a very sensible person. You
wouldn't do anything wacky . . . would you?" He had
a hopeful expression in his eyes.

Jana tried to look as innocent as possible. "Wacky?
Not me. My mother has always told me I'm the most
sensible teenager she knows. She trusts me."

"That's great," said Marco, looking relieved.

"That's why when I call her tomorrow and tell her I
want to stay on Barbados a while longer, I'm sure she'll
go along with it."

"WHAT?" exclaimed Marco. "You're kidding. She wouldn't let you."

"Oh, yes, she would," said Jana. "You see, she married this rich newspaper man named Wallace Pinkerton, and they like to do a lot of things together. I'm just kind of in the way sometimes. She wouldn't mind. I'll tell her there's a good private school that I can stay at here."

Jana had her fingers crossed behind her back as she talked. What she was saying wasn't totally a lie. Her mother *was* married to a newspaperman. Of course Pink was just a Linotype operator and certainly wasn't rich.

"Have you told anyone about our meetings?" he asked, looking at her closely.

"Me? Tell? You told me not to," she answered in an innocent voice. "Do you *want* me to tell?"

He waved his hand to dismiss the idea. "No, no," he said, then looked up at her seriously.

"Jana, I'm a lot older than you. How old are you? Thirteen? Fourteen? I'm sixteen. That makes me three years older than you."

"So what?" Jana retorted. "My mother's five years younger than Pink."

Marco's shoulders slumped.

"You know what!" Jana said, jumping up. "I think

I'll go call Mom right now. Then I can tell you what she said tonight at the New Year's Eve party."

"Great," said Marco sarcastically. "Can't you at least just wait until tomorrow? It'll give you more time to think it over. It'll give *me* more time to think."

"I can't wait!" said Jana cheerfully. "But you can go ahead and think anyway. I'm going to do it right now." She turned and ran back up the slope to her bicycle.

Melanie had never in her life seen a person looking as dejected as Marco was when she arrived at Sand Dollar Beach. His face was so long she thought his chin would touch the sand, and his eyebrows were puckered together in worry.

She took a deep breath. Then dancing happily around Marco, she cried, "What a beautiful island! What a beautiful day! Come on," she said, taking him by the hands and pulling him up. "Don't look so gloomy."

"I can't help it," he responded. "I've been running into too many cheerful people."

"Maybe I can lift your spirits."

"Oh, no," said Marco, turning away. "Here comes another one." He turned around again quickly. "You're going to tell me that you're going to run away so you can stay here on Barbados, or that your mother's rich and doesn't mind if you stay here and go to school."

"Oh, no!" said Melanie, trying to look surprised. "Why in the world would you expect me to say that? My parents wouldn't let me stay, and my mother certainly is not rich."

Marco shook his head, looking slightly relieved. "You wouldn't want to know," he said, shoving his hands into his pockets.

"But I did write a letter to my boyfriend, Scott Daly, and told him I don't want to go with him anymore."

"You did what?" Marco asked in alarm.

Melanie braced herself to tell the story she and the others had made up for her. "I told my boyfriend from home, Scott Daly, that I don't want to go with him anymore. After being with *you*, he seems so immature." Melanie leaned against Marco. "And even though I have to go home tomorrow, I know I can come back. My dad says we've got a distant cousin who works for the big oil company here. I'm sure I can talk my family into letting me come and stay with cousin Milton and his family. In fact, I left them a note suggesting it before I came here to meet you. They'll have read it by the time I get back."

"Have you and your friends been talking about me?" Marco asked, looking suspicious.

"Sure we talk about you, but I didn't bring up the fact that you and I have been meeting." I didn't have to, Melanie added silently. The truth came out.

"Oh," said Marco.

"Let's walk out in the water and collect sand dollars," said Melanie. "I want some to take home and put them around my room so that every time I look at one, it'll remind me of you."

Marco followed her despondently out into the water.

Katie throttled back the Jet Ski as she neared the Sand Dollar Beach. It had been a longer ride from the rental area than she had expected, and she was about to give up and turn back when she saw the big rock sticking out of the water. She guided the machine expertly in a smooth arc toward the beach. Marco was up by the road tinkering with his motorcycle. He turned when he heard her run the Jet Ski up on the beach.

"Hi," she called as she walked up to him.

"Hello," he answered quietly.

"What are you doing?" Katie asked, pointing to the motorcycle.

"I need to get back to the hotel. Tonight's New Year's Eve, remember? I have to get ready for the party." He sounded angry.

"You wouldn't have left without seeing me?" she asked, pretending to be surprised. From what the other girls had told her, Katie had half-expected Marco to be gone when she got to the beach.

"No. I wouldn't," he answered. "I'm anxious to know what your plans are."

"My plans?"

Marco looked at her as if he was considering what to say next. "Never mind," he finally said.

"Marco?" Katie said timidly.

"Yes?"

"Are there islands around here were there aren't any people?" she asked.

"Sure, I suppose so."

"Are they hard to get to?" she continued.

"No."

"Are there coconuts and fruit and other things you can eat growing there?"

Marco looked at her closely. "There're coconuts and pineapples and other kinds of fruit on all the islands. Why?" he asked suspiciously.

Katie raised her head and looked him squarely in the

eyes. "Can you get there on a Jet Ski?" She thought she saw his face twitch nervously.

It was a moment before he answered. "Yes."

"I don't want to go home tomorrow," she said quickly as she threw her arms around his neck. "Can't we take two Jet Skis and escape to an island so I can stay with you?"

Marco slowly peeled her arms from his neck. "No, we can't," he said with a sigh. "I've got to go." He turned, climbed onto his motorcycle, and kick-started it.

"But what about us?" asked Katie over the *braaackkk* of the bike's engine.

Marco just shook his head and drove off.

Katie stood watching him go with a gleeful expression. It was great seeing Marco's terrified look, she thought, even if I did have to throw myself at him!

CHAPTER

15

"*I get to stay up till midnight!*" yelled Jeffy to Melanie as she and the rest of The Fabulous Five came into the villa. He was swinging a clackety noisemaker around in the air.

"We'll see about that, young man," said Mrs. Edwards.

"I wouldn't worry about it," said her husband, winking. "He hasn't stayed awake past ten o'clock yet."

"Dad," Melanie asked, "would it be all right if we called Scott, Keith, Tony, Randy, and Jon to wish them happy New Year?"

"I suppose so," said her father. "But keep it down to no more than three minutes each."

"Thanks, Daddy!" Melanie said, standing on her tiptoes to kiss him on the cheek before she and her friends hurried out of the room.

The outside dining area was decorated with multi-colored crepe-paper streamers and balloons. Dinner was finished, and people were chattering happily as they listened to the band, and Jeffy was clacking his noisemaker as hard as he could.

Whenever Melanie's parents weren't looking, The Fabulous Five took turns making eyes at Marco as if to tell him he was the greatest male in the universe. He would answer with a weak smile, but it was clear that he was becoming more and more uneasy.

"Remember, really play this up," instructed Katie. "If he's scared now, just wait until we get through with him."

The girls nodded to each other in agreement, their pact sealed. Next they took turns going to the girls' room and walking close to the stage as if they were going to whisper something to him. Whenever Marco saw one of them coming, he would suddenly have to adjust an amplifier or talk to one of the musicians.

"I'm almost starting to feel sorry for him," Jana whispered.

"Don't," said Katie. "He deserves everything he's getting."

"It'll be over for him soon enough," said Christie, referring to the last part of their plan.

"He is a good singer," offered Melanie.

"You should have seen his face when I told him I wanted to stay here and join the band so I could sing with him," said Beth. "He looked absolutely green."

"He looked the same way when I showed up on a Jet Ski," said Katie. "I bet he never wants to see any of us again."

As the evening went on, everyone got anxious for midnight. The Fabulous Five danced all night long, each taking a turn with Mr. Edwards.

"De Congaline!" yelled Marco as the band broke into the familiar song.

The Fabulous Five had been waiting anxiously for this moment, and they jumped up and quickly formed the head of the conga line. Jana was in front, followed by Christie, Beth, Katie, and Melanie. Other people tagged on, and the line grew as they wound their way in and out of the tables.

The crowd clapped and cheered as Jana led the line from one end of the dining area to the other and then

24-32-22

PORTLAND HIGH SCHOOL

1100 IONIA ROAD

Dedication

Sunday, September 30, 1990

out onto the dance floor. Slowly she led them back and forth across the floor in long snakelike curves, getting closer and closer to Marco. As the head of the conga line came toward him, each of The Fabulous Five put on her biggest and best smile.

Marco seemed to panic. His voice got softer and softer as he sang the words to the calypso song, and his eyes grew wider with alarm. The closer the line came, the more worried he looked.

Finally Jana led the line up onto the stage. Marco began backing up, and she cornered him against one of the drummers. Then, giving him a sinister look, she reached into her pocket and pulled out her sand-dollar necklace.

Marco's eyes grew wide and he gulped as she reached up and put the necklace over his head. Then she danced away into the crowd.

Behind Jana, Christie twirled her necklace in front of his face before she slid it over his head where it hung beside the first one. She, too, whirled away from the conga line and left Beth facing him. One by one, each of the Fabulous Five placed her necklace around Marco's neck until he stood, mouth open, wearing all five.

The expression on his face as he looked back at The Fabulous Five said it all. He had been caught at his game, and he knew it. After that Marco avoided looking at The Fabulous Five.

The girls spent the rest of the evening waiting for the midnight fireworks display. Melanie's father had been right about Jeffy. No matter how hard he tried, his eyes got heavier and heavier, and he was sound asleep on his mother's lap well before the clock reached midnight.

The hotel had positioned a clock over the stage for the occasion, and as the second hand approached twelve, everyone in the audience started counting.

"SEVEN!"

"SIX!"

"FIVE!"

"FOUR!"

"THREE!"

"TWO!"

"ONE!"

Cheers went up as skyrockets shot into the air, exploding in fire storms of colors. The band started playing "Auld Lang Syne," and people jumped from their seats and hugged and kissed each other. The Fabulous Five yelled, "Happy New Year," hugging each other and Mr. and Mrs. Edwards.

After the party ended, The Fabulous Five went back to their villa, put on their p.j.'s, and pulled chairs up into a semicircle on the patio. None of them wanted the evening to end. When it did, their vacation on Barbados would also be over.

Finally, Katie broke the silence. "What a fun vacation," she said, watching some pale clouds float across the sky.

"I'll say," agreed Beth. "Even though Marco pulled his dirty tricks on us."

"He really took us for a ride," said Melanie.

"It was mean of him to do the things he did, but I think maybe I understand why he did it," said Christie.

"You do?" asked Jana. "Why?"

The others turned to hear what Christie had to say.

"Once when I asked him about hangouts on Barbados that tourists didn't know about, he told me that there are only so many places you can go on an island, and he had been to them all a million times. He said, like Magnum, P.I. says on TV, 'Another boring day in paradise.' Everything he does has to do with people who come here from someplace else."

"One time when we were talking," Beth added, "he said that the *Peg Leg Pete*, the boat that takes people out to party, was for rich tourists like me. He told me he is usually in the water with the rest of the guys selling Jet Ski rides."

"I think Marco's bored and resents everybody having

a good time while he has to work," said Christie. "Flirting with each one of us was his way of creating some fun for himself."

Jana pulled herself upright in her chair. "You know, I've been thinking, too. He couldn't have done it if we hadn't wanted him to."

"What do you mean?" demanded Katie. "He's the one who fooled us. He even had us arguing with each other. He had to know that there was a chance of breaking up our friendship."

"We did get carried away," said Christie. "I mean, here we are on a beautiful island in the Caribbean. And the singer in the band is the most gorgeous guy we've ever seen. How romantic can you get?"

"I've got the best boyfriend in the world at home," said Jana slowly. "But I forgot about Randy when an older boy paid attention to me. What kind of loyalty is that?"

"I even forgot about Scott and Shane," said Melanie.

"That means you were twice as bad as the rest of us," said Beth. The Fabulous Five laughed as Melanie took a playful swing at Beth.

Katie stretched as far as she could to reach the over-head baggage compartment where she'd stuffed her carry-on bag and jacket. She wasn't tall enough, so she put one foot on the seat and then reached it easily.

Christie had seen snow piled on the sides of the runway when the plane taxied to its gate, and she hoped her coat would be warm enough. What a change from the warm, sunny Barbados weather, she thought.

Jana was digging her purse and bag out from under the seat in front of her, and Beth and Melanie were in the aisle organizing their things. They were talking excitedly about whom they were going to call first to tell about their vacation.

"You know what," said Beth, looking at her friends, "I can't wait to get home."

"Me either," said Jana. "I'm going to call Randy as soon as I get in the door. I didn't realize how much I missed him until I talked to him yesterday. The more I think about what a super guy he is, the more of a dummy I know I am after what happened on Barbados."

"I haven't decided whether to call Scott or Shane first," said Melanie. "I want to tell them *all* about Barbados at the same time."

"Maybe you can set up a conference call with all three of them," said Katie, grinning.

"Ha, ha," said Melanie, "very funny."

"Double-check to make sure you're not forgetting anything, girls," called out Mrs. Edwards.

"We have, Mom," Melanie assured her.

The passengers filled the aisle and started moving slowly toward the exit.

The Fabulous Five walked forward with everyone else and finally made it to the aircraft door and into the Jetway leading into the terminal. As they reached the end of the tunnel, they stopped dead in their tracks. Standing in front of them were Randy Kirwan, Keith Masterson, Tony Calcaterra, Scott Daly, and Jon Smith.

"*Welcome home!*" yelled the boys.

The girls shrieked and made beelines for their boyfriends, throwing their arms around their necks.

"We missed you," Randy said, smiling at Jana.

"Yeah!" said Scott, grinning at Melanie. "I've never been so bored in my life."

"Yo, Your Honor," Tony said to Katie. "It's good to have you back."

"It's wonderful to be back," she said, looking up at him.

"Did you guys have a good time?" asked Jon.

"Yes," answered Jana. "We had a great time."

"I hope that doesn't mean you met a bunch of guys," said Keith.

The Fabulous Five looked at each other.

"We *definitely* did not meet a *bunch* of guys," said Christie quickly.

"Yeah," said Beth, taking Keith's arm, "you can count on that." She winked over Keith's shoulder at the other members of The Fabulous Five, and each of them winked back.

CHAPTER

16

"**W**ow! Is this ever going to be a wild and crazy weekend," Melanie shouted to her friends as she hurried up to the fence where they were standing before school on Wednesday morning. Her face was glowing. "Friday night is my big date with Shane. And then, on Saturday, my Grandma Edwards is coming to stay with us for a while. In fact, she may live with us permanently. Isn't that great?"

"Is it?" asked Jana. "I mean, I know your date with Shane is great. You haven't talked about anything else since he asked you out. But are you really excited about having your grandmother come to live with you?"

"I was wondering that, too," said Christie. "My grandmother is in a wheelchair, and life gets really complicated when she comes for a visit."

"Not my grandma," Melanie assured them. "I can't wait for you to meet her. She isn't . . . well, *elderly* like some grandmas. She's really lively and she likes to be involved in things. She likes to water-ski and go camping. Last summer she even went parasailing. And she'll like Shane, too. I *know* she will."

"Hey, maybe you should change your date to Saturday night so she can go along," teased Katie.

"Right," added Beth. Then in a high-pitched voice she imitated Melanie. "Close your eyes, Grandma Edwards, while I kiss Shane good night."

Everybody giggled except Melanie. "You guys can laugh all you want to, but my grandma *could* go along on a date. She's that great!"

But what will Melanie do when Grandma Edwards gets a little *too* involved in things and seems about to wreck Melanie's love life on the most romantic day of the year—Valentine's Day? Find out in The Fabulous Five #22: *Melanie's Valentine*.

Meet Taffy Sinclair!

If you're a fan of The Fabulous Five series, you'll love the Taffy Sinclair books by Betsy Haynes. That's where Jana, Katie, Christie, Melanie, and Beth form The Fabulous Five in order to keep up with the snootiest (and prettiest) girl in their class—Taffy Sinclair. In these funny stories about The Fabulous Five's adventures before they start junior high school, Taffy Sinclair stops at nothing to outdo Jana and the rest of The Fabulous Five. She tries blackmail, starring in a TV soap opera, and even being friendly, but together The Fabulous Five manage to stay one step ahead of their archenemy, the perfectly gorgeous, perfectly awful Taffy Sinclair!

You can follow The Fabulous Five's fifth- and sixth-grade adventures and find out how it all started in these Taffy Sinclair books available from Bantam Skylark Books:

The Against Taffy Sinclair Club

It was bad enough when Taffy Sinclair was just a pretty face. But now that she's developing faster than Jana Morgan and her four best friends, it's all-out war! What Jana and her friends don't know is that even the best-laid plans can backfire suddenly.

Taffy Sinclair Strikes Again

It's time gorgeous Taffy Sinclair had a little competition. That's why Jana Morgan and her friends form The Fabulous Five, a self-improvement club. But when the third club meeting ends in disaster, Jana finds she has four new enemies. And with enemies like these, there's only one friend worth having . . . Taffy Sinclair!

Taffy Sinclair, Queen of the Soaps

Taffy Sinclair has done it again! This time, she's landed a role in a soap opera, playing a beautiful girl on her deathbed. Is there any way at all for The

Fabulous Five to fight back against Taffy Sinclair, the TV star?

Taffy Sinclair and the Romance Machine Disaster

Taffy Sinclair is furious when she finds out that Jana Morgan is the first girl at Mark Twain Elementary School to have a date with Randy Kirwan. Taffy gets her revenge when their sixth-grade teacher conducts a computer matchup game and nine other girls beside Jana turn out to be a "perfect match" with Randy!

Blackmailed by Taffy Sinclair

Taffy Sinclair has never been *this* terrible! When Jana finds a wallet that turns out to be stolen property, and Taffy catches her with it, Taffy makes Jana her personal slave. Jana is stuck serving Taffy her lunch, carrying her books, and worst of all, being her friend, until the rest of The Fabulous Five can help her prove her innocence.

Taffy Sinclair, Baby Ashley, and Me

Jana and Taffy are on their way to the principal's office after having an argument in class when they find an abandoned baby on the front steps of the school. The two girls rescue baby Ashley, and become overnight celebrities. But can two archenemies share the limelight?

Taffy Sinclair and the
Secret Admirer Epidemic

Jana Morgan has been receiving love notes from a secret admirer! And when Taffy Sinclair finds out, she's sure to be jealous. The Fabulous Five set out to uncover the identity of Jana's secret admirer . . . and uncover a big surprise instead.

Taffy Sinclair and the Melanie Make-Over

When Taffy Sinclair tells Melanie about a new modeling school, Melanie talks The Fabulous Five into signing up. Soon Melanie is spending lots of time with Taffy Sinclair, who's promised to get Melanie professional modeling jobs. The Fabulous Five know Taffy's up to something. . . . Can they win Melanie back when Taffy's holding out the lure of a glamorous modeling career?

The Truth About Taffy Sinclair

Taffy finally gets her chance to tell the story of the rivalry between her and The Fabulous Five. It's the last week of sixth grade at Mark Twain Elementary School, and all the students are cleaning out their lockers. When some of the boys switch around everyone's belongings, most of the kids think the prank is funny. For Taffy Sinclair, however, it's no laughing matter. Her personal diary is missing, and now the whole school will learn the truth about Taffy Sinclair!

Now Taffy Sinclair is back, in a book all her own titled *Taffy Sinclair Goes to Hollywood*.

Here is a scene that takes place *before* Taffy goes to Hollywood:

By the time Saturday morning arrived, and Taffy and her mother rode the commuter train into New York City, Taffy was so excited that she could scarcely breathe. She had done lots of auditions for television commercials, but this was her first movie audition. Her biggest break. Channing Crandall *had* liked her improvisation. Maybe she would get the part and go to Hollywood, after all. The thought made her tingle with excitement.

They took a cab to the building on Fifth Avenue where the audition would be held. It was ten minutes to one when they arrived, and Taffy's audition was set for one o'clock.

"Go on, honey. Go on in," her mother urged.

Taffy slowly opened the door to the waiting room and went inside. There were at least a dozen girls already there with their mothers, and more than half of them were standing because there weren't enough chairs. Taffy looked around and started to panic. Almost all of them were brunettes! There was only one other blonde, and she wasn't really a blonde. Her hair was medium brown with streaks of blond. Why am I here? she wanted to cry. There must be a mistake!

Mrs. Sinclair had noticed it, too. She bent close to Taffy's ear and whispered, "Don't worry, sweetheart. We can always dye your hair if you get the part. Remember, Mr. Crandall liked you. Just be yourself and do your best."

Taffy took a deep breath and crossed the room to the desk, aware that everyone was looking her over, sizing up the competition, and definitely noticing that she had blond hair. She quickly put her name on the union sign-up sheet and handed her résumé to the smiling woman behind the desk.

"Here are your sides, sweetie," said the woman. "You are auditioning for the role of Tiffany Stafford." She handed Taffy a couple of pages from a script that she would be using in the audition and then turned back to her typewriter. She hadn't even seemed to notice that Taffy was a blonde.

"Thanks," murmured Taffy. This was really it. Behind her, she could hear some of the other girls talking together.

"I did *six* auditions this week," a short brunette with huge brown eyes was saying. "My agent says I'll probably get so many offers that the producers will have to bid on me."

"But aren't you putting on a little weight?" asked a slender brown-haired girl standing next to her. "I would think being overweight would limit the number of parts you could play."

Taffy winced at the girls' catty remarks. This was really cutthroat competition—at least in the waiting room. She clutched the sides and looked for a place to stand where she could have some privacy. She had to forget about the other girls and the color of her hair and study the lines she would be reading for Channing Crandall. What if she got them wrong? Or got her tongue twisted? What if he was sorry he had invited her to audition? She remembered what Merry Chase had taught them in acting class: "*Don't memorize the lines because then if you forget them you'll blow the audition. Just get familiar enough with them so that you won't have to keep your eyes glued to the page.*"

Taffy picked out the speeches that belonged to Tiffany Stafford and tried to study the lines, but she couldn't concentrate. Her eyes kept darting nervously to the door beside the secretary's desk. It was the door to the audition room, and every so often a brunette would come out, and then the secretary would stand and read off the name of the next girl on the list.

Taffy peered over the top of her sides, watching the faces of the girls coming out for clues to how the auditions were going. Not one of them was smiling.

A chair scraped across the floor. "Taffy Sinclair," called the secretary.

Taffy froze for an instant, but she could feel the eyes of all the others girls on her. All those brunettes who wanted the part as badly as she did. All of them hoping she would panic and run away without even auditioning. Well, she wasn't going to give them that satisfaction. She squared her shoulders and went to the audition-room door. Then she opened it and walked in. She could hear her heart pounding in her ears. Channing Crandall was standing in the center of the dimly lit room talking to the man behind the video camera. In front of the camera was a pool of light, and Taffy knew from experience that was where she would stand.

"Come on in, Taffy," the casting director said cordially, his silver hair catching the light. "It's good to see you again."

Tossing one last frantic look over her shoulder at her mother who had to stay in the waiting room, she closed the door and tried to return Channing Crandall's smile. Her mouth felt starch-stiff. Do I look scared? Will he be able to tell how nervous I am? She moved into the light and faced the camera before she could lose her nerve.

"Before you begin," said the casting director, "let me tell you a little about the story we are filming. *Nobody Likes Tiffany Stafford* is the story of beautiful Tiffany whose life is made miserable by three best friends who despise her. They do everything they can to turn the rest of the school against her."

Taffy tried to keep her mouth from dropping open and from letting the shock she was feeling show on her face. NOBODY LIKES TIFFANY STAFFORD! she wanted to shout. That sounds like my life in Mark Twain Elementary when Jana Morgan and her friends had a club against me called The Against Taffy Sinclair Club!

Find out what happens when Taffy gets the part and goes to Hollywood in *TAFFY SINCLAIR GOES TO HOLLYWOOD*.

ABOUT THE AUTHOR

Betsy Haynes, the daughter of a former newswoman, began scribbling poetry and short stories as soon as she learned to write. A serious writing career, however, had to wait until after her marriage and the arrival of her two children. But that early practice must have paid off, for within three months, Mrs. Haynes had sold her first story. In addition to a number of magazine short stories and the Taffy Sinclair series, Mrs. Haynes is also the author of *The Great Mom Swap* and its sequel, *The Great Boyfriend Trap*. She lives in Marco Island, Florida, with her husband, who is also an author.

Some things are for grown ups.
Some things are for kids.
But the best things are **Just For Girls** **Petite Naté**

Like *The Fabulous Five* and *Caribbean Adventure*,
Petite Naté™ is created especially for you.

A fragrant cologne to splash or spray-on, bubbles
and shampoo to turn your bath into an adventure, plus
talc and lotion for after-bath fun–it's all **Petite Naté**.
And it's all Just For Girls.

Happy Holidays to all our friends!

Love,
The Fabulous Five
Jana, Melanie, Beth, Christie and Katie

Offer available in U.S.
Jean Naté* Petite Naté™ © 1990 Revlon, Inc., Dist., N.Y., NY 10022

AN173

Taffy Sinclair is perfectly gorgeous and totally stuck-up. Ask her rival Jana Morgan or anyone else in the sixth grade of Mark Twain Elementary. Once you meet Taffy, life will **never** be the same.

Don't Miss Any of the Terrific Taffy Sinclair Titles from Betsy Haynes!

Follow the adventures of Jana and the rest of **THE FABULOUS FIVE** in a new series by Betsy Haynes.